DUSTY AYRES AND HIS BATTLE BIRDS:
THE SCREAMING EYE

THE SCREAMING EYE

By Robert Sidney Bowen

ALTUS PRESS • 2017

EDITED AND DESIGNED BY

Matthew Moring

PUBLISHING HISTORY

"The Screaming Eye" originally appeared in the October, 1934 (Vol. 6, No. 3) issue of
Dusty Ayres and his Battle Birds magazine. Copyright 2017 by Steeger Properties,
LLC. All rights reserved.

CHAPTER 1
PHANTOM MURDERS

FOR THE fifth time in the last two blocks, Dusty Ayres stopped and gazed at the array of miscellaneous merchandise in a store window. This time it happened to be a tobacco shop, but Dusty noted that fact absently. His main reason for stopping was to shoot a flash glance back over his right shoulder. And as he did the tiny frown on his brows deepened, and his lips came together in a thin, grim line. He was very troubled.

The short, shabbily dressed civilian had also stopped. This time he bent over and retied his shoelace.

With impulsive decision Dusty walked into the store and over to the glass-topped counter.

"Something you'd like, captain?" beamed a bald headed clerk who slid forward.

"Package of Haig Curly Rub," grunted the pilot.

"Certainly, captain. And perhaps you'd like—"

Dusty didn't hear the rest. Out of the corner of his eye he had spotted the face that peeked around the edge of the door for a split second. The civilian was sticking close.

"—And there's certainly been a lot about you in the papers, captain. I'm very proud to be able to serve you."

Dusty started.

"Eh? Oh, yes, thanks." Then, bending over the counter, he lowered his voice. "You have a rear door to this place?"

The clerk blinked.

"Why—er—yes, of course. Is there anything wrong, sir?"

Dusty shrugged.

"That's what I want to find out," he mumbled, and moved down the counter. "Make as though you want to show me something out back," he added under his breath.

The clerk looked mystified, but he nodded, nevertheless.

"Certainly, captain," he said in loud tones. "If you'll just step this way, I'll show you what we have."

Bowing and smiling, the clerk ushered him through a door, and when it had closed behind them, he pointed across a stockroom.

"It's over there, sir," he said. "Can I be of any help? I don't quite understand."

"Neither do I," replied Dusty. "But thanks, and stick here for a couple of minutes, will you?"

Without waiting for the clerk's reply, he walked swiftly across the room, and shouldered through the rear door. It brought him out into a small court, with a narrow alley leading to the main street.

Feet barely making a sound on the pavement, he slid down the alley, eased around the corner and stopped dead. The short civilian was there with his back to him, and not four feet away.

A quick step and he tapped the man on the shoulder.

"Waiting for someone?"

At the sound of the voice the civilian whirled. Dark eyes flashed, and the fingers of the right hand twitched convulsively—actually crooking, as though pulling a gun trigger. Then, just as rapidly, the stranger relaxed and a nervous, embarrassed laugh spilled off his lips.

"Why, er—yes, sir," he gulped out. "I was waiting for you. As a matter of fact, I've been following you for some time."

"I know you have!" cut in Dusty, in a hard voice. "So, what's it all about, eh?"

"Why, er—" the civilian stammered. "As a matter of fact, Captain Ayres, I've been trying to get up enough nerve to ask you for your autograph. I'm collecting the signatures of famous people. Now, if you'll be good enough to—"

"Drop your hand!"

THE WORDS whipped off Dusty's lips like machine-gun

4

bullets. The civilian's right hand, reaching for his inside jacket pocket, shot down stiff and straight at his side. His eyes widened in a flicker of momentary fright.

"I—I don't understand," he managed to gasp.

"No?" the pilot snapped. "I think you do. Now listen, I don't just get what it's all about, and I haven't the time right now to find out. But, you're a pretty bum actor, mister, and this time you lose. Don't move!"

Before the other had time to blink an eyelash, Dusty snaked a hand under the left lapel of the man's jacket and pulled out a small, snub-nosed automatic. Hefting it carelessly, he fixed agate eyes on the short fellow.

"Trying to get up enough nerve, is right!" he cracked. "About face, you! We'll tell it to that cop over there on the corner. Get going!"

The dark-eyed civilian started to protest, but it began and ended with a sharp yelp of pain as steel fingers clamped down on his shoulder and spun him around. With a doglike whimper he started walking.

The policeman didn't notice them until they had reached his side. Then he saw Dusty and snapped a salute. But when his eyes swept over the short man they narrowed, and the muscles of his face tightened.

"You, eh, you little rat?" he barked. Then to Dusty, "What's the charge, captain? He been panhandling you? He's 'Hand-Out' Hicks, and a gutter rat if there ever was one!"

The civilian seemed to shrivel up under the policeman's glare.

"I ain't done nothing!" he whined. "I ain't done nothing, and that's the truth!"

Dusty handed the snub-nosed gun to the cop.

"He's right in that," he said grimly. "I took this away from him before he could do anything. He's been following me for the last five or six blocks."

The policeman looked from the gun to Dusty's face and back to the gun again. His eyes were wide with dumbfounded amazement.

"Well, I'll be a—" he gasped. He turned to the short man, "Back on stick-up work, hey? Well, you punk, you'll get plenty for this. Thanks, captain. Will you be down for charges in the morning?"

Dusty nodded.

"Yes. If it's necessary."

Answering the policeman's salute, he turned on his heel and retraced his steps down the street. The frown was still on his brow, and there was a puzzled look in his eyes.

"Now what in hell did that little mug think I had that was worth stealing?" he muttered to himself.

After a few moments he gave it up with a shrug, turned down a side street and headed toward a High Speed Group 7 car, which was parked at the next corner. Lounging against the door was a tall, curly-haired flying lieutenant, a cigarette dangling from between his lips. On official records he was listed as Lieutenant C. B. Brooks, but to Dusty and the rest of the 7th Group, he was just plain "Curly."

As he spotted Dusty he spat out the cigarette, straightened up and waved his hand impatiently.

"Shake it up, kid!" he yelled. "What am I supposed to do—wait all day? I've got everything, and what I haven't, is being sent out."

Without waiting for an answer, he slid into the front seat. Dusty lengthened his stride, came abreast of the car and got in behind the wheel.

"Some mug tried to stick me up," he grinned. "And—look out, Curly! Down!"

Even as Dusty shouted the warning and hauled the other down onto the car floor, spitting flame zipped out from a doorway thirty yards up the street and the air reverberated with the savage rattle of sub-machine-gun fire. Metallic darts hammered against the side of the car, and the windshield became criss-crossed with a million fine cracks.

So suddenly had come the burst of fire and so suddenly had it ceased, that even as its yammering died away to an echo, men and women on the sidewalks were still continuing to their respective destinations. And then as the realization of danger flashed to them all, they became panicky and either froze to the spot or went screaming for shelter.

It all took no more than four seconds. But at the ticking of the fifth second, Dusty was out of the car and racing up the street, right hand tugging at his holstered automatic. Upon reaching the doorway he ducked in only to be brought up short by a stoutly built door that was securely locked. And as he was debating the idea of shooting away the lock, a siren wailed its eerie note and a radio police patrol car jerked to a screaming stop at the curb.

"Hey, what's this all about? Whatcha doing with that gun?"

Dusty turned to meet the sharp questioning eyes of a patrol sergeant. In a couple of crisp sentences he explained.

"Why, search me!" he finished. "By chance I happened to spot the gun—a sub—swinging my way. My pal and I ducked just in time. Whoever did it, is in this building somewhere. But I intend to find out. I don't like being shot at."

THE PATROL sergeant gave him a quizzical look, eyed the door a moment, then stepped forward and tried it. By that time a couple of beat-men came lumbering up. They saluted the sergeant and stared at Dusty, and at Curly, who had joined his pal.

"Well?" Dusty finally snapped. "Do we all stand here and let him get away?"

The sergeant didn't like that, and his face showed it.

"How do you know they—or him—was shooting at you?" he got out gruffly.

Dusty jerked a thumb toward the Group car.

"That's plain enough, isn't it?" he barked. "Now, I demand that you search this house—right now!"

Perhaps it was something in Dusty's voice, or perhaps it was the look on his face. Anyway, the sergeant nodded to the beat-men and told them to smash in the door. A minute or so later the hinges gave way, and the wood crashed in.

"Just a minute, captain!" snarled the sergeant, as Dusty started to bound inside. "This is a police job. We'll go first." With a beat-man outside to send the gathering crowd away, the rest went into the house. It took but a flash glance at the cob-web-covered walls and stairway to realize that the place was vacant. And as they mounted to each of the five floors their original belief was simply confirmed. From cellar to flat-topped roof they found nothing but cobwebs and at least twenty years' collection of dust.

One thing, however, Dusty noted before any of the others and he pointed it out to the sergeant. The trap skylight was not bolted, and a scattering of dust showed that it had been recently opened.

But the sergeant was not much impressed. He simply shrugged his shoulders and brushed dust particles from his uniform.

"Doesn't mean anything," he grunted. "Lots of bums use these joints to flop in. They come in and go out by the trap, here. But, I'll make a report, anyway," he added grudgingly. "Just leave me your name for the records, and I'll see that the place is watched."

Ten minutes later, Dusty and Curly were back in the car. And a minute after that, they had nudged through the gaping crowd and were on their way out to the 7th's temporary airdrome, just a few miles north of Springfield, Mass.

"Holy gosh!" exploded Curly. "Some welcome home for you, kid. What the hell do you make of it? There wasn't any fooling about that fellow trying to get us. Boy, that sergeant was one dumb cop!"

Dusty only grunted and shrugged. Eyes fixed on the road ahead, he tried to figure out an answer. The only thing he gained was a firm belief that Hand-Out Hicks had not had stick-up ideas in mind. He had trailed Dusty to shoot. And failing in that, someone else had taken up the job. Why?

For a moment he thought of Black Invader agents, but dismissed the idea as ridiculous. To begin with, Hicks was not a Black. He was an American crook; a native of the lower strata. IT COULDN'T possibly be Black agent work. Hell, after three rotten weeks in the hospital he'd only rejoined the Group that morning. Hadn't even taken up his new ship yet. The gang had insisted upon a celebration, and he and Curly had driven in town for a few needed liquid supplies.

"Maybe I'm goofy!" he muttered aloud. "But I can't see any yeggs shooting us up for the bit of change we might have."

"You're wrong there, kid," spoke up Curly. "Only a week ago a couple slugged Bert Jones, of the Fifth, in an alley and took him for his last five bucks. This war is a gold mine for the underworld rats—at least those that have evaded the first draft. Oh well, they missed us. So what the hell! Come on, a little more speed!"

It was then that Dusty realized that he had unconsciously slowed down to a snail's pace. Feeding hop to the thirty-two small bore cylinders under the streamlined hood, he sent the car rocketing down the broad highway. Driving with inborn ease, he slid around traffic, beat a dozen or so traffic lights by the fraction of a second, and eventually swung off onto the narrow dirt road that led directly to the field.

Engine purring a song of mighty power, and wheels spewing up a cloud of dust, Dusty swung the car around a sharp bend, straightened out—and it happened.

Not forty yards ahead, a big car, of ancient vintage, shot out from behind a group of trees, bounced to the center of the road and came to a full stop. Curly's bellow of alarm deafened Dusty as he slammed on the brakes. And the shrill screaming of rubber tires striving frantically to grip the dirt, added to the bedlam of sound.

In the split seconds allowed, Dusty saw that the big car was empty, and that he had less than four feet of clearance on either side. A crash was inevitable.

"Hang on, Curly—I'm going to the left!"

Hands locked about the wheel, he swung it down hard, snapped off the brake, and thumped his foot on the gas. Rear end swaying crazily, the car shot half off the road, and roared straight ahead. A split second later there was a terrific roar of sound as the right front bumper smashed into the left front wheel of the car blocking the road.

The jar of impact flung Dusty side-wise, and for a fleeting moment his hands started to slip off the wheel. But he grabbed it again and hung on for dear life, as the heavy Group car knocked the other vehicle clear over on its side. They went crashing past amid the screeching sounds of ripping metal.

"Clear!" shouted Dusty. "We're—"

He never finished the rest. At that moment, just as they were about to tear into the clear, the swaying rear end of their car slammed up against the other auto, and their right rear wheel buckled.

Like a derailed express, the Group car fell off on the right side. Then, as though boosted by some invisible giant's hand, it careened over the opposite way and went plowing crazily into the woods. In the flicker of time left, Dusty flipped off the ignition, flung both arms up over his head and put every bit of his weight on the brake pedal.

A tree trunk slammed into the front wheels, and everything became a blurred volcano of thundering sound as the car went whirling over on its back; over onto its crumpled wheels again— and over some more. A spinning world of darkness and sound.

CHAPTER 2
KIDNAP PILOT

FROM A thousand miles away, Dusty heard Curly Brooks' shouting voice. "Hey, kid—hey! You all right?"

The sound of the voice pried open his eyes, and it was then that he saw he was still sitting in the car. Or rather, still sitting in what was left of it.

The top had been ripped off as though slashed by some great knife. The engine hood was like crumpled paper jammed around a split tree trunk. And the engine, itself, was resting crosswise on its bearers. But, thanks to armor plating, the sides of the car were intact.

Dully, Dusty realized that the armor plating had contributed a good deal to the fact that they were still alive. He grinned cheerfully at his flying pal.

"A couple of bumps here and there," he said. "But I guess that's all. And you?"

The other cursed roundly.

"I don't dare find out," he finished up. "Good God, who the hell do you suppose ran that car onto the road?"

The question clicked like steel in Dusty's aching head. Thankfulness at still being in one piece had made him momentarily forget about the real cause of the accident. Like a shot his hand flew to his gun. He bent close to Brooks.

"He must still be around, Curly," he said in a low voice. "I've a hunch he wants to make sure. We'll nail him and find out a few things. Damned if this isn't getting to be a habit!"

Making as little movement as possible, they eased out of the car, crept into some bushes, and waited. They sat there well over fifteen minutes before a twig snapped some distance off to their right. Brooks started crawling, but Dusty grabbed him and shook his head.

"This is good enough," he whispered. "Wait until he shows himself!"

Bodies crouched and ready to spring, eyes narrowed and glued in the direction from which the sound had come, they waited another minute or so. And then a bush moved some twenty feet beyond the wrecked car and a checkered cap came into view. Below it was a face!

The mouth was thin and tightly drawn. The nose was mashed a bit to the left of its original position. And the skin was like faded yellow paper, pock-marked and taut.

But it was the newcomer's eyes that attracted the two Yanks most. They were dark, deep-set, and glowing with a weird, fiendish light—the kind of light that comes into the eyes of a ruthless killer just after he's got his man in the back.

For a moment the checkered cap and the face beneath it were motionless. Then the bush parted, and a thin, flashily dressed man stepped out, and sneaked close to the car. Clutched in his grimy right hand was a big .38 revolver.

"Hold it, you!"

Dusty's words rang out like three distinct pistol shots. The stranger froze for an instant. Then he whirled and jerked up the gun. Like a flash, Dusty dropped, and pulled his own trigger as he went down. The killer screamed, his gun leaped from his

DUSTY DROPPED AND PULLED HIS OWN TRIGGER.

clawing fingers. But almost instantaneously Curly's gun roared, and the man spun around like a top, then fell flat on his face.

"Hell!" snorted Brooks, as Dusty scrambled to his feet. "Trying for his shoulder, and I think I killed him."

In five seconds they found that out for sure. The man was stone dead. Dusty's bullet had smashed his gun hand wrist, but Curly's had plunked right through the heart.

"Sorry, kid," he apologized. "I guess I didn't help much with my bum shooting. He'll never tell us anything."

Dusty didn't answer. Instead, he bent down, rolled the fast stiffening figure over and started a search of his pockets. He could well have saved his time. Apart from a few bills of low denomination, and a colored silk handkerchief, he found nothing. AS HE was getting to his feet again, there came the roar of a car tearing down the dirt road at terrific speed. Hardly had they both recognized it, than they heard the screeching of brakes.

On mutual impulse they raced through the bushes just in time to see another one of Group 7's cars come to a dead halt a bare four feet from the wrecked car of the killer. A corporal driver was behind the wheel, and as he came jumping out of the door his face as white as brand new paper.

Dusty recognized him immediately.

"Corporal Sharron!" he yelled, breaking into a run.

The non-com spun around and stood gaping, eyes like saucers and jaw sagging.

"Gosh, sir!" he gulped as Dusty pulled up. "W-w-what happened? I damn near ran into it, sir."

"We had a little trouble, corporal," the pilot answered. "Listen, our car's wrecked. I want you to take us to the field at once. You've got room to turn here."

"Sure, sir," the other was still gasping. "Was on my way to fetch you, sir, anyway," he continued. "You're wanted at the field at once. Major Drake sent me. Said I'd find you in town."

"Anything wrong?" asked Dusty, as he and Curly climbed in the back of the car.

"Don't know, sir," the non-com told him. "But a couple of medicos—colonels, sir—landed in an ambulance plane about fifteen minutes ago. Had an escort of four pursuits. Right after that, the major told me to hunt you up."

Dusty scowled and leaned forward.

"Ambulance plane?" he echoed. "Just repeat all that, will you, corporal?"

The man did, practically word for word. Dusty sank back and stared at Curly Brooks.

"How in hell did they know we might be needing an ambulance?" he grunted.

His pal shrugged, gingerly fingering a goose egg on the side of his head, and sighed.

"Think up your own answer," he grumbled. "After what's happened so far—I expect most anything. But, I will say this. Someone's sore at you, or me—or both of us. Damned if I know! Ooh, my head!"

With a groan Brooks leaned back and closed his eyes. Elbows on knees and doubled fists as a rest for his chin, Dusty stared straight ahead, searching for an answer. But, there was none forthcoming. And by the time Corporal Sharron braked the car to a gentle stop in front of Group 7 H.Q. shack, all he had was a more painful headache.

He promptly forgot his head as he jumped out of the car and shouldered in through the door. Behind the desk sat Major Drake, and on his left were two moon-faced colonels of the medical corps.

At Dusty's entrance, Major Drake glanced up, frowning. But his frown immediately vanished as he saw his ace pilot, and a look of alarmed amazement spread over his wind-bronzed face.

"For God's sake, Dusty!" he exclaimed. "What in the name of all that's holy happened to you?"

When Dusty had finished telling him, the expression on the C.O.'s face had changed to one of marked consternation. The two medical officers were also alarmed. And although Dusty was not sure, he thought that they exchanged a swift glance of mutual agreement about something.

"Good God!" gasped Major Drake when he found his voice. "I can't understand it. But, by the Lord Harry, I'll have a few words to say to the Police Commissioner, later. Heaven knows we're having enough trouble with the Black Invaders, not to be bothered with a lot of highway crooks and killers."

"But what was there for them to steal?" Dusty cut in. "If I was a paymaster, on the way back from the Area field cashier, I might understand. And if they had been Black agents out to win a medal or two, I could also understand. But they weren't. Both of the men I saw were common, every day gunmen. Just cheap killers, without much guts."

"Pardon, major," one of the medicos suddenly broke in as

Dusty stopped. "We're in a hurry, you know. And if you don't mind, we'd like to—"

"Yes, certainly, colonel," the C.O. nodded. And then to Dusty, "These gentlemen are Colonel Watts and Colonel Standish, Dusty. They constitute a special medical board sent up from Washington H.Q. They want to examine you to see if you are ready yet for a return to active service." Dusty saluted and grinned.

"**I CERTAINLY** appreciate Washington's concern over my health, sir," he smiled at the one introduced as Colonel Watts. "But I guess they didn't know that I had a medical board exam at the hospital this morning, before I left. And I was pronounced in tip-top shape. The little experience I've just had didn't do any serious damage. No, I'm perfectly fit, sir."

The colonel addressed shrugged.

"Nevertheless," he said evenly. "We're here to examine you. Now, if you'll just take off your clothes, we'll—"

"But why all the trouble, sir?" Dusty questioned stubbornly. "I'm perfectly all right. And you said that you were in a hurry, so there is no sense taking up your time."

"Our orders are to examine you, captain," replied the other firmly. "Please take off your clothes."

Dusty's jaw tightened.

"But, it's ridiculous!" he exclaimed.

"It's an official order, Dusty," Major Drake broke in smoothly. "Here, read it."

He tossed a square of paper across the desk. Dusty grabbed it up and glared at the typed words.

19

Major A.P. Drake, C.O.
H.S. Group 7.

Sir:

Colonels Watts and Standish, of Staff Medical Unit, have been appointed a special board to examine Captain Ayres and determine if he is physically and mentally fit for return to active service. You are hereby ordered to accept their judgment as final, and abide by any decision they deem necessary for the good of Captain Ayres, and the service in general.

> Signed, L.B. Bradley,
> General,
> Officer Commanding
> U.S. Air Force.

As Dusty read the note over twice a queer sensation rippled through him. Just why it was, he didn't know. There was no doubt that the order was official—he recognized General Bradley's signature at once.

But, why the hell go to all this bother, when Washington G.H.Q. must know that the Boston Military Hospital wouldn't have discharged him unless he was fit? Hell, didn't Bradley trust Boston medicos?

With a shrug, he tossed the order back on the desk.

"Very well," he sighed. Then he added grimly, "But I hope the couple of cracks I got on the head, in that car smash-up, won't mislead you. I really feel better than I ever have before in my life."

Three minutes later he stood before them naked. The two

medicos took various instruments from a little black bag, and went silently to work. From head to foot they pounded and thumped him, and listened attentively through binaural stethoscopes. They examined his ears, his eyes, his nose, and his mouth. Took blood pressure readings; made him hop about on one foot, then on the other, and recorded heart-beat fluctuation.

In short, they couldn't have done any more if they'd cut him apart and examined him piece by piece. And all the time they made notes and figures on half a dozen different charts.

Winded, aching all over, and getting madder by the minute, Dusty nevertheless was patient. Finally they stepped back and nodded.

"You can get into your clothes now, captain," said Colonel Watts.

Then after a brief glance at Colonel Standish he turned to Drake.

"We are taking Captain Ayres to the Washington Base Hospital for observation," he said quietly, "Unfortunately, there is a peculiar heart and lung condition that will bear watching."

Had a bomb exploded at that instant Dusty would not have been more startled.

"What?" he roared, forgetful of rank. "To Washington Base for observation? Like hell I'm going to Washington Base! Why, I—"

Colonel Watts spun on him, and his ordinarily quiet voice cracked like a whip.

"Silence, captain! You forget yourself. We are here under orders from G.H.Q. and you will abide by our commands! Is

21

that clear? Do you think we have any personal desire to keep you away from active duty, after all the wonderful deeds you've accomplished? Of course not!

"You are a very valuable man to the Service, and G.H.Q. does not wish to take any chances. Now please go and gather what few things you wish to take along with you."

"But, colonel," Dusty began, then stopped. "How long will I be confined for observation?" he finished with a groan.

"That, I cannot say," Colonel Watts replied in a more kindly tone. "It all depends on developments. A week, perhaps. Maybe more. Now, please hurry, captain."

DUSTY HESITATED, but as he caught a strange look and a short nod from Major Drake, he turned on his heel and went out. Fists bunched, chin on chest, he plodded over to his hutment and stuffed a few things in a bag. Ten minutes later he came out.

The two medicos and Major Drake were standing by the ambulance plane. The plane's prop was ticking over slowly. Four staff pursuit ships were already taxiing out onto the field, pre-paratory to taking off.

Stopping a moment, Dusty watched them streak down the runway and zoom up into the blue. Taking his eyes off them he looked down the tarmac of his own field. His chin squared stubbornly, and a glint of sadness mingled with the anger in his eyes.

Lined up wing-tip to wing-tip were the twenty-one planes of High Speed Group No. 7. And the one nearest him was his own ship—Silver Flash III. His ship—and he hadn't even test flown it yet! It was a special model of the Barling XFB type, in which were incorporated several radical improvements that he himself had recommended to the engineers.

The Silver Flash III had been the only thing that had made him stay that third week in the hospital. It hadn't been finished at the end of the second week, and so he had succumbed to the medicos and stayed. But those last seven days had been days of dreams—dreams of the Silver Flash III and of the day when he would take it up and find out what it could do. And now—

He groaned a curse, tore his eyes from the sleek, glossy craft and shuffled over to the ambulance plane. When he reached the group he saluted stiffly.

"Ready sir," he muttered to Colonel Watts.

The senior officer nodded, started to climb aboard when Major Drake stopped him.

"I'd like to have a few last words with Captain Ayres, colonel."

And before Watts could reply, Drake took hold of Dusty's arm and led him out of earshot.

"Listen, son," he said in a low voice. "Don't take it too hard. I think there's more to this than either of us imagine." Dusty stiffened.

"I don't get you, sir!"

"Then, listen," grunted the other. "Five minutes ago I got Bradley on the wire—G.H.Q. official wire. Told him about your experience today, and said I didn't think it was a fair time for you to be examined. Incidentally, I wanted to check on that order of his—though I've heard of Watts, I've never met him. See what I mean?

"Well, anyway, when Bradley heard what had happened to you—the shooting, I mean—he hit the roof. Fairly yelled orders for you to be flown to Washington Base Hospital at once. Wouldn't answer any of my questions—just kept on yelling for you to be flown there immediately. Then there was a click, and the line went dead."

As Dusty listened, the queer sensation returned to him, only this time about twofold stronger. He gave his C.O. a searching look.

"And you think, sir?" he questioned softly.

The other shook his head.

"I'm not thinking," he replied, tightening his grip on Dusty's arm. "I've only got a hunch—a hunch that you won't be in Washington Base Hospital for very long. So—no, don't question me, I don't know the answers. Just keep your chin up, and see the thing through. And, luck!"

Dusty gripped Major Drake's hand, then went back to the ambulance ship, climbed in and took a seat just back of the sergeant pilot at the control. The non-com grinned recognition, licked his lips in momentary nervousness at performing in front of Uncle Sam's top eagle, then steadied down and hand-heeled the twin throttles open. The engines picked up and the ambulance plane roared down the runway, gathered speed and nosed up into the clear air.

Slouching back, Dusty gave the two medicos but a passing glance, then closed his eyes and silently mulled over what Major Drake had told him. Headed for Washington Base Hospital—and what?

He didn't know. Nor did he know that at that very second, far up above the cloud layer, a cruel-eyed figure was dropping a pair of fog-penetrating binoculars back into their cockpit rack and enjoying a harsh, rasping chuckle.

CHAPTER 3
VANISHED PATROL

AFTER HAVING been able to answer none of his own questions, Dusty finally opened his eyes. Leaning toward the compartment window, he stared down at the squared panorama of ground sliding by. Absently he noted that they were flying down across Connecticut and would pass New York City.

A sudden desire to see what the great city looked like after the unsuccessful Black attack made him turn to the pilot to ask him to fly over it. But, as he put out his hand, the signal light on the radio panel blinked rapidly and the compartment speaker unit cracked out words.

"Lieutenant Barber calling Ambulance Sixteen! Emergency! Keep as low as possible—enemy flight has been sighted. Will try and drive them off, but keep low altitude in case they break through. They—oh, my God—what's that?"

A split second after the sharp exclamation, the speaker unit emitted a blood-chilling scream—weird and eerie, with a faint throbbing note to it. It was not like the scream of a human being in mortal pain. There was something mechanical about it—more like the screaming of an over-revving generator grinding its bearings to shreds for lack of oil. Or like a high speed express racing around a sharp curve with all wheels locked.

But regardless of what it sounded like, it came blasting out of the speaker unit and made the blood of every man in the cabin run cold. For a second no one moved. They sat like stone images, eyes glued to the speaker unit, as though it were some powerful magnet they could not resist.

And then with a hoarse curse Dusty leaped to his feet and grabbed the sergeant pilot.

"Call him back full volume!" he snapped. "And find out what happened. Dammit, man, snap into it!"

Like a mechanical doll suddenly set into action, the non-com shot out his hand, spun the wave-length dial and put the transmitter tube to his lips. His voice was almost blanketed out by the ear-splitting scream of sound that still came over the air.

"Lieutenant Barber on seven-eight-ten!" he bawled. "Lieutenant Barber on seven-eight-ten. Message cut off. What has happened? Signal back on wave-length four-two-five!"

Three times the man repeated the message as Dusty and the now white-faced medicos, waited breathlessly for Lieutenant Barber to speak again. But, as the seconds dragged by, no human voice was heard, and the unearthly sound increased in pitch.

On sudden impulse, Dusty reached out and snapped off the speaker unit, and turned to Colonel Watts.

"Barber is leading that staff pursuit escort of yours, isn't he, sir?" he asked.

The medico gulped and nodded.

"Yes, yes, of course, it's Barber!" he got out in a shaky voice. "Good God, what do you suppose it is? I never dreamed we'd be attacked—I wondered why they sent an escort, too. Sergeant, head for Washington as fast as you can!"

"Hold it!" barked Dusty as the non-com started to nose down for speed. And then to Watts, "What's one of the other pilot's wave-length?"

"Wave-length?" echoed the other dully. "Why, I'm sure that I don't—"

Dusty ignored him and snapped the question at the sergeant. He received the answer almost before he got the question out.

"Lieutenant Kress is on ten-two-four, sir. And Lieutenant Stubbs is on three-nine-seven. Shall I try them, sir?"

"No!" barked Dusty, taking hold of his arm. "Out of the seat, Sergeant! I'll take over!"

"Here, captain, stop that!" cracked Colonel Watts, suddenly coming to life. "I ordered the sergeant to fly to Washington as quick as he could. Our orders are to—"

"Orders be damned for the moment!" Dusty flung at him angrily. "There's trouble upstairs and my job is flying. You can take me to your blasted hospital later."

"You heard Colonel Watts' order, didn't you?" roared Colonel Standish, sticking his oar in for the first time. "My God, man, are you crazy? There aren't any guns on this plane. You'll get us all killed!"

"Who said anything about guns?" Dusty ripped back at him, reaching for the wave-length dial. "If those chaps are in trouble, it's up to us to notify the nearest field and have help sent up. And I'm going to find out. Now, be quiet, all of you!"

PULLING THE nose up with a jerk that made both the medicos grab frantically for support, he spun the dial to Lieutenant Kress' reading and snapped on the speaker unit.

"Kress—emergency!" he yelled into the transmitter tube. "Report activity at once. What's your altitude? Where are you? Send report and we'll relay for help. Ambulance Sixteen calling you!"

Once again every eye was unconsciously glued to the speaker unit. That is, every eye but Dusty's. He had snapped on the head-phones, and his eyes were glued to the signal blinker on the dash.

But not once did the light blink, and not once did a voice

sound in the earphones. Even the screaming noise was no more. On either side of the long nose of the ambulance ship the props clawed the air and engine vibration transmitted a faint purr back into the sealed cabin. But, apart from that, there was dense silence.

Four times Dusty called Kress, and four times he waited expectantly. Then he switched to Stubbs' reading and frantically repeated his call. But all to no avail. It was as though the escort planes above the cloud layer never really existed.

"See here, captain, see here!" Colonel Watts shouted. "Perhaps you do not obey orders, but we do! And our orders are to take you to Washington Base Hospital—and take you there at once. Now, I demand that you turn over the controls to the sergeant!"

Fire in his eye, Dusty turned slowly and faced him.

"I don't disobey orders, colonel," he said evenly, "unless it's necessary for me to do so. And this happens to be one of those occasions—I think.

"Our escort has run into trouble. What, we don't know. But, it's our job, at least, to find out. Now, if you don't like—well, there's a couple of chute packs on the cabin wall there. You and Colonel Standish can bail out!"

Colonel Watts' jaw dropped and his eyes flickered over to the chute packs in their wall racks. The sight of them seemed to further unnerve him. White-faced, eyes wide, he sank down into his seat. Colonel Standish had preceded him to his own seat by perhaps one half of one second.

Turning forward again, Dusty concentrated on getting as much climb out of the ship as possible. The cloud layer was at twenty-five thousand, a good ten thousand above them. And the heavy ambulance plane was struggling bravely toward it.

Eventually the ship reached it, nosed into the misty whiteness, and presently nosed out again into clear air. Hunching forward over the Dep wheel, Dusty strained his eyes and carefully searched the surrounding skies, but he saw nothing.

Leveling off, he gave the sergeant pilot the nod to look, too. Between them they covered every square inch of air space within range. The result was the same—just empty air.

For the want of something to do next, Dusty spun the wave-length dial and in turn called Barber, Kress and Stubbs. But the signal light on the dash panel refused to blink, and he received nothing but ringing silence.

Completely mystified, and feeling not a little foolish for having taken things into his own hands, Dusty swung the plane around in a series of ever widening circles. And it was when he was halfway around on the tenth circle that the signal light blinked and words crackled in the ear-phones.

"Washington H.Q. calling Ambulance Sixteen—emergency! Are you still in the air? Report your position at once, and another escort will be sent from nearest local field. Ambulance Sixteen—report your position at once."

SHOOTING OUT his hand, Dusty started to spin the wave-length dial to the Washington H.Q. reading, when suddenly he glanced at the directional receiving-wave dial, and stiffened. The small, delicately balanced needle was pointing a few degrees southwest.

A glance at his dash told him that he was flying due east.

That meant that according to the directional dial some station other than Washington H.Q. was on his wave-length. If it was Washington, the directional needle would be pointing due south, if not just a few degrees east of south.

Letting his hand drop, Dusty carefully rechecked his readings. He was right—Washington was not on his wave-length. Some other station that knew Ambulance 16's wave-length reading was faking a Washington H.Q. call.

Besides, how did Washington know that the escort had been destroyed—if it had been destroyed? There were four ships in the escort—four chances for an S.O.S. signal to have been sent out. And as an S.O.S. went out over every wave-length, Ambulance 16's set couldn't possibly have missed picking it up. That is—unless the ambulance ship had been blanketed out.

As the last raced through Dusty's mind he thought of the eerie screaming sound in the speaker unit. Had that queer noise been the blanketing out signals? He shook his head vigorously.

"Like hell it was!" he grunted aloud to himself. "I've heard blanketing out signals. That damn sound was caused by something else."

"Answer them, captain! Answer Washington H.Q. What are you waiting for?"

Colonel Watts' voice rasped against Dusty's ear-drums like a file. The Yank spun around angrily to explain his doubts. But as he opened his mouth, he had a sudden inspiration, and he clicked his teeth shut.

"In a minute, sir," he said instead. "I've got to check our position first."

As he spoke the last, he nosed the ship down in a steep dive, and went slicing through the cloud layer. The instant he came into clear air he studied the ground, and checked with the roller map on the dash. Finally satisfied, he spun the wave-length dial to the Washington H.Q. reading and picked up the transmitter tube.

"Ambulance Sixteen calling Washington H.Q.!" he shouted. And before a check-back signal had time to come through, he continued. "We are still in the air, at map position K-Twelve and flying south by west. Please rush escort to replace one destroyed by enemy aircraft. Emergency! Send escort at once!"

With a quick movement, he snapped off the set and nosed back up into the cloud layer. A sharp exclamation to his right caused him to turn his head and stare into the puzzled eyes of the sergeant pilot.

"But, skipper!" the non-com gaped. "We're not at K-Twelve! That's almost fifty miles west of us. Look, here, on the roller map!"

"I know!" Dusty checked him in a low voice. "But that wasn't Washington H.Q. calling us. You just sit tight."

"Not—" the other began, and finished with a nervous gulp. "But what are you going to do, skipper?"

"Find out a few things," replied Dusty calmly, as they broke through the top of the cloud layer. "Some one wants to know where we are, so we just reversed it and let Washington H.Q.

know where they are—or where they'll be damn soon. It would be just my luck to be flying a lumbering crate like this!"

"And no guns!" the non-com finished huskily.

Dusty nodded grimly. Then nosing the ship down just a bit, so that it was almost buried in the crest of the fleecy cloud layer, he sent it loafing in a southwesterly direction at half throttle. Holding it steady with one hand, he picked up the cockpit binoculars with his other and adjusted them to his eyes.

Then began an eternity of waiting. It seemed as though the heavens themselves had ceased all motion and were waiting breathlessly for the unexpected to happen. Three times Dusty felt Colonel Watts' hand on his shoulder, and heard him demanding the reason for such crazy flying. But he paid no attention to the senior officer. Simply shrugged off the hand and kept the binoculars glued on the distant and empty skies.

Five minutes dragged by—and became ten, then fifteen. But still the skies remained empty of everything save thin blue air and endless, rolling layers of fleecy whiteness.

Dusty's eyes ached from the strain of looking at the same spot for so long a time. He had to battle furiously with himself not to close them and give them the rest they needed. But he dared not—not even for an instant.

From head to toe, he was gripped with a peculiar belief that something strange—something almost unreal—was hovering high up in the blue. And he wanted to be able to see it the very instant it showed itself.

THEN SUDDENLY, he spotted a tiny group of dots far to the south. The dots had raced up through the cloud layer, and as he peered at them, he saw them level off and swing in the general direction of map position K-12.

A few seconds later they took on the definite silhouettes of seven biplanes. And then, as the sun's rays glanced off the glossy fuselage of the plane in the lead, he saw the markings of the 10th Pursuit Group.

Washington H.Q. had picked up his call and relayed it to the 10th, located at Binghamton, N.Y.—the nearest drome to map position K-12. A flight of the 10th lads had gone streaking into the air. There they were now, swinging out into line formation, each pilot undoubtedly searching the heavens for a plane he couldn't see.

Unconsciously, Dusty gripped the Dep wheel more tightly, his thumb feeling vainly about for the reassuring touch of a trigger trip lever. At that moment, a heavy hand fell on his shoulder and the voice of the sergeant pilot rang in his ears.

"Look, skipper, up there! Black ships coming down!"

Taking the binoculars from his eyes, Dusty glanced upward and to the right. Rushing down in a wing-whining dive were ten Dart monoplanes of the Black Invader Air Force.

His eyes went agate as he saw them, but a moment later a perplexed frown creased his brows, and he unconsciously switched his gaze south and toward the American ships. He could see them clearly now without the binoculars. They were still in line formation and flying a westerly course—at right angles to the diving Blacks!

"What the hell!" he exclaimed in amazement. "Don't they see each other?"

...THE TWO END PLANES.... DISINTEGRATED INTO A MILLION SMOKING PIECES...

That, evidently, was the case, for not a single plane in either of the two flights changed its course a hair. The Blacks went plunging down toward the north, and the Yanks still roared along to the west.

Hardly realizing that he was doing it, Dusty spun the wavelength dial to the S.O.S. reading and snatched up the transmitter tube.

"Tenth on patrol!" he roared. "Tenth on patrol. Enemy planes diving north of you! Enemy planes...."

He didn't finish the rest, for at that instant the Yank patrol swung sharply to the north and closed up in attack formation. But the Black ships kept right on diving down.

They were at least a good seven or eight thousand feet above the American planes, and in an ideal position for battle. Yet, they completely ignored the Yank ships and stuck rigidly to their original course.

"Go get 'em, Ten!" Dusty howled. "They don't even see you. Oh, God—if I only had the Flash under me!"

Their prey sighted, the Yank planes seemed to virtually leap through the air. In a twinkling of an eye they closed up the intervening distance. Then, in perfect co-ordination—as though one hand held all of the throttles—the American formation zoomed up, and jetting flame spewed out from the stream-lined nose of every ship. As though anticipating the maneuver, the Blacks careened sharply off to the right and roared into the clear with less than a split second to spare.

Around went the Yanks after them, props savagely clawing the air, and every gun pumping out a continuous stream of lead.

Boiling with rage at not being able to take part in the fight, Dusty was nevertheless filled with pride at his flying mates' performance. Outnumbered by three planes, they were putting the enemy to wild and frantic rout. Like curs with their tails between their legs, the Blacks were "grabbing air" in a desperate effort to break free from the bullet spitting eagles on their tails.

"Get 'em, Yanks!" bellowed Dusty. "Close up—you can do it! You—"

He finished the rest in a choked cry of alarm. Frozen rigid in the seat, he gaped wide-eyed at a spot in the heavens above and behind the pursuing Yanks.

Something—a crimson blur was rushing downward. It had no silhouette, no shape—just a streak of red cutting down across the sky. Powerless to move, he sat there watching it with eerie fascination.

Suddenly it happened.

A long fan-shaped beam of yellowish green light spewed out from the front end of the crimson blur. The speaker unit of Dusty's plane emitted a blood-curdling, screaming sound, and before his horrified gaze, the two end planes of the Yank formation disintegrated into a million smoking pieces—went showering down into oblivion.

CHAPTER 4
CRIMSON HELL

" **G**OOD GOD—WHAT is that—look at the thing!"
Dully, Dusty was conscious of Colonel Watts' babbling voice in his ears. As a matter of fact, the sergeant pilot
and Colonel Standish were also crying out frantic, incoherent
questions. But he paid not the slightest attention to them.

Every bit of his attention was riveted on the eerie phenomenon of death which was sweeping down from the upper alti-
tudes. To his dazed eyes it was still only a blur of crimson out
of the front of which spewed the fan-shaped ray of light. But
as a third American plane melted apart in mid-air, the diving
phantom altered its position and took on definite shape and
outline. It was the strangest craft of the air Dusty had ever seen,
or even dreamed of seeing.

To begin with, it was a low-wing, twin-engined monoplane.
The engines were faired into the wing on either side of a pointed
snout, and so close to the stubs that there was but a few inches
of clearance between the prop-tips and the side of the nose.
There was no landing gear axle; single landing struts supported
the wheels, each of which were encased in long stream-lined
"pants."

The fuselage and tail section were of conventional design.
That is, with the exception of the turtle-back of the fuselage.
And it was that part of the plane that jerked an amazed gasp
from Dusty's throat.

Directly over the center of the wing-span, and three or four feet back of the engine, was a small turret such as one sees on the top of armored cars. The front part was slotted, as though for a traversing machine gun.

But there was no machine gun there now. Instead, there was what seemed to be a great, big, yellowish green eye that cast out a long fan-shaped beam. And even as Dusty stared at it spellbound, he saw it sweep from side to side, just as a human eye moves in its socket.

A great, yellow-green eye, that cast its glance down across the sky and destroyed all that it touched. Like a gigantic blow-torch, it melted the Yank planes one by one. And all the time it gave forth that horrible screaming noise that had been picked up on Ambulance 16's radio and amplified to deafening proportions.

Suddenly, like the turning of a switch, the great eye winked out. Instantly the screaming sound died away to an echo, and with a thundering burst of speed, the strange craft zoomed high and lost itself to view in the sub-strata zone.

Save for Dusty's wild shout no one made a sound in the ambulance plane cabin. Like men drugged, they stared out at the smoking debris of seven American planes slithering down out of sight. Then, as though by mutual signal, they all turned and gaped at each other.

"You saw it? They're gone—gone. And—we might have gone, too. They—"

Colonel Watts' mumbled words ended in a choking sob. Dusty took hold of his arm, and shook him none too gently.

"Get hold of yourself, colonel!" he barked. "This is no time to pass out!"

The medico raised his bleary eyes, stared at him as though he were seeing a ghost.

"You might have got us all killed!" he moaned thickly. "By God, I'll report you for this, Captain Ayres. Disobey a senior officer's orders, will you?"

"And I shall most certainly substantiate the colonel's report!" broke in Standish excitedly.

Bust Dusty ignored them both. A great cloud of shame had enveloped him. He, Dusty Ayres, had been responsible for sending of seven men to their deaths. He had sent them roaring after the bait in a terrible sky trap!

True, he had done it unwittingly. He had only followed the course any other pilot would have under the circumstances. He had found mystery in the air, and had tried to solve the enigma of the lost escort. But, at the moment, he blamed himself for everything.

HEARTSICK, HE let the loafing plane have its head, and stared out across the fleecy crest of the cloud layer. Inside his brain a thousand and one unanswerable questions spun about. One moment he tried to assure himself that he had simply awakened from a terrible nightmare. The next, he was filled with a savage desire to ram his lumbering crate upward and search out the crimson destroyer.

But, before he had a chance to do either, the sergeant pilot yelled sharply, clawed at his shoulder with one hand and pointed upward with the other.

"Skipper—look. It's spotted us—and it's coming down. For God's sake, skipper—let's get out of here!"

As Dusty jerked his eyes upward, he saw the crimson plane slicing downward. A split second later its fan-shaped beam spewed outward, the tip sweeping across the top of the cloud layer, toward them.

Sight and action became one for Dusty. He thumped down on right rudder, and at the same instant flung his weight forward on the stick.

"Hang on!" he roared, "We're going down!"

Whether they heard him above the din from the speaker unit, he did not know. Nor did he pause to find out. He was too busy hand-heeling both throttles open, and virtually throwing the big lumbering craft into a wing-screaming dive.

As though chained to the top of the cloud layer, the ambulance ship bucked and sawed against Dusty's vicious movements. Then with a sudden lunge, it mushed over on right wing and cut down into the enveloping mist. But, as it sliced in, a brilliant light hissed past its wing-tip, and to Dusty it seemed as though he had been plunged into a blast furnace.

"It's got us!"

The sergeant pilot howled like a wild animal trapped in a landslide. He clutched wildly at Dusty's shoulders, and babbled like a maniac. With a curse, Dusty hit him under the jaw and knocked him sprawling on the cabin floor.

"Let go, you fool!" he panted. "Or we'll never get out!"

Face grim and jaw set, he fought to keep the big plane in its mad spin downward. The cloud layer had become a seething inferno, through which a finger of death groped for its victim.

Dusty realized vaguely that distance, and only distance, had saved them. Just the tip of the mysterious yellow-green beam had touched them. And undoubtedly there had not been sufficient power in it to more than scorch them.

Now the pilot of that crimson plane was combing the cloud layer for them—searing the fleecy whiteness in an effort to find them.

Distance! That was what he needed—as much distance as possible between the ambulance plane and the crimson destroyer. That the other ship could out-dive him, he knew. His only hope lay in losing himself in the clouds, and then scudding out when he had a chance.

Had a chance? God, when would that be? They were flying through what seemed like liquid fire. The Dep wheel he grasped was red hot. He was breathing flame, and his lungs felt ready to shrivel up with the heat.

At any second the fuel tanks might let go. Already, the engines were pounding dangerously on their bearers from the furious over-revving of the props. And with each flickering second he caught a glimpse of that weird, fused beam swinging about in the clouds around them. Now to the left, now in front, and now to the right.

"There it is again dead ahead! It's sweeping toward you! Bank—bank! No—the other way! It's swinging around. Too late—"

Dusty choked back the babble of words that spilled off his

lips with a groan, he cut both engines and stared helplessly at the light sweeping through the clouds.

And then, at the very instant he had steeled himself for the finish, the light faded out, and the screaming speaker unit went silent.

LIKE A half drowned man who has been pulled from inky waters at the last moment, Dusty sucked breath into his aching lungs, and leaned back against the seat rest. Sweat poured off his face, and every stitch of his clothing stuck fast to his clammy body.

But the reaction that set in lasted only a moment. With an effort, he pulled the plane out of its wobbling spin and brought it up to a gentle gliding angle. A split second later—as though a giant hand smashed against it—the plane keeled over on left wing, and slid once more into a crazy spin. Again he pulled it out, and again it flopped right back into a spin.

Then, as it screwed down out of the clouds and into clear air, Dusty saw the cause of the new danger that faced them all. A good two feet of the left wings had been melted away, and both the upper and lower ailerons were gone.

Even more important was the fact that half of the left elevator and a small part of the rudder had also been burned and melted away. In short, barring a miracle, the ship was doomed to crash.

Dusty saw all that in the flash of a second. Steeling himself, he deliberately looked at the altimeter and then at the ground below. They were twenty thousand feet up and just a shade east of the foothills of the Appalachian Mountains.

Position and altitude checked, he half turned his head. "Sergeant!"

A hand touched his shoulder and a voice mumbled thickly. "Y-y-yes, skipper?"

"How many chute packs, sergeant? I noticed only two."

"That's all, sir," came the answer. "There should be more, but they—"

Dusty cut him off with a curse.

"Save it!" he snapped. "Sergeant, help the colonels get into those two chutes. And when I yell, jam open the door and let them bail out. Better open the door first. I don't know how long I can hold this damn thing steady."

As Dusty finished a figure bent over his left shoulder, and Colonel Watts' fear-widened eyes glared into his.

"What—what's that you're saying?" he shouted. "Bail out— I've never jumped in my life. Can't you land this plane? Good God, captain—"

"No, I can't!" Dusty shut him off. "The controls were burned away by—that thing. And we've only got two parachutes. The sergeant and I are pilots, so you two officers can have the chutes."

"But, good God!" the other shouted, "I don't want to jump, and our orders were to—"

"To hell with your orders!" Dusty roared at him. "My God, I'm trying to save your life! Get back there and let the sergeant help you into that chute. He'll tell you how to use it. Get back, I tell you. I'm in command of this plane, now!"

Dusty had half risen from his seat as he bawled out the order, and the look on his face must have impressed Colonel Watts with the belief that bailing out was the lesser of two evils. For, with face a shade more chalky, he hastily stumbled back to where the sergeant was pulling the packs out of their wall racks.

Calling upon every bit of his flying skill, Dusty battled the controls of the plane in a desperate effort to keep it from whipping into a tight spin. Time after time he pulled it out with split seconds to spare, and brought the nose up only to have it drop right back into a sluggish spin again. And then, after what seemed a lifetime, he heard the sergeant pilot's voice.

"Ready with Colonel Watts!"

Without bothering to look back, Dusty pulled the nose up to a fluttering stall.

"Out he goes!" he roared.

He heard a yelp of fear, and then through the cockpit window he saw the spread-eagled figure of Colonel Watts go skidding off into space.

Seconds later, he saw the chute folds shoot up from the pack, and he grunted with relief. "Catching" the stall with a bit of engine, he sent the big plane sliding off on wing.

"And again, sergeant!" he shouted.

Once more he heard a yelp, and once more he saw a flapping figure sail outward and down. Then the chute silk spewed upward and mushroomed out.

"What's our chances, skipper?"

DUSTY TURNED at the casual question and looked into the sergeant pilot's eyes. They were steady and unwinking—not a trace of fear in their depths. He reached out his free hand and pressed the man's arm.

"Set your own odds, sergeant," he grinned. "I don't know, but I'll do my best."

After he'd pulled the ship out of another two turn spin, he spoke again.

"Sorry there were only two chutes, sergeant. But the medico's rated them both. We're pilots, you know."

The non-com gave him grin for grin.

"Oke with me, skipper," he said. "I'll string along with you. But what do you suppose that damn thing was? My God, those boys didn't stand a chance. That thing must have gotten the first escort, too. How can a guy scrap a thing like that?"

Dusty shrugged, and his face went hard.

"I don't know," he muttered. "But, if I come out of this I'll find a way! I owe that much to those lads. Now, get aft, sergeant. Your extra weight on the tail may help. When I yell, grab hold and hang on. Luck, buzzard!"

The non-com's face beamed as Dusty washed aside rank and called him the pilot-to-pilot nickname.

"And luck to you too, buzzard!" he sang out heartily.

Dusty grinned, then turned and squinted at the ground below. What he saw didn't cheer him up any. They were over a range of rugged foothills—just the nastiest sort of section in which to make a landing with a decent plane, to say nothing of a crippled ship. But the thought of the strange crimson aircraft fired him with grim determination.

Hand steel-steady, he reached out and spun the wave-length dial to the S.O.S. reading.

"Emergency, all ground stations!" he yelled into the transmitter tube. "Ambulance Sixteen about to crash at map position K-Nine. Ambulance plane about to crash at map position K-Nine! Controls badly damaged. All stations listening in, please send assistance at once to that point. S.O.S. signals from Ambulance Sixteen!"

Repeating the message three times he snapped off the set and steadied himself for the last five hundred feet. With luck he might be able to mush down into the trees, belly first. If he could do that, the branches would take up some of the shock. But if he couldn't— He shrugged and left the question unanswered.

As he switched off the engine and pulled the throttles all the way back to check fuel leakage, the signal light on the dash panel blinked furiously. The thought that perhaps his S.O.S. signals had been jumbled, and ground stations were calling for a check-back, made him flip the switch and spin the dial. He did it with one swift movement, for there were only seconds left. Tree tops were reaching up toward him like spear-shaped fingers.

"Ambulance Sixteen!" he yelled hastily. "We are crashing at map position—"

He stopped with a gasp as a harsh voice in the ear-phones cut in on him.

"Our regrets, Captain Ayres. We would much rather have seen you die in the sky!"

With a sharp click the ear-phones went silent.

Dusty gaped at the radio panel. Then the slight jar of the

right wing-tips "crabbing" on the topmost branch of a tree, snapped him back into action.

"Hang on, sergeant!" he bellowed, and hauled back on the stick with all his might.

The big plane quivered and trembled from prop to tail wheel. It seemed to float sidewise, then with a *swo-o-o-sh* it dropped like a stone.

A world of firecrackers exploded about Dusty. A myriad of brightly colored balls of light danced and whirled before his eyes. And then a great curtain blotted out everything, and he went plunging down into a canyon of utter silence.

CHAPTER 5
DEAD MAN'S SECRET

LIQUID FIRE passing down Dusty's throat pried open his eyes. He was sitting in a chair in a white-walled room.

A young army medico was taping up his left wrist, and someone was holding a whisky glass to his lips.

He coughed, pushed away the hand holding the glass and looked at its owner. He found himself staring into the shaggy-browed eyes of General J.T. Horner, chief of U.S.A. Intelligence, He blinked in amazement.

"You, sir?" he choked out. "Why, what—?"

The other's eyes flashed a warning, and he stopped short.

"Take it easy, Ayres!" snapped the big man. "Don't talk. Here, have some more of this."

Obediently, Dusty took the whisky glass and slowly drained

it to the bottom. The tingling liquid cleared his slightly fogged brain and filled him with a new and glowing sense of strength.

Without a word the general took the empty glass from his hand, placed it on a nearby table, and then stood straddle-legged, hands clasped behind him, and watched the young army medico finish taping Dusty's wrist.

BLACK HAWK

Presently the medico grinned and nodded.

"There, captain," he said. "It's just a slight sprain, and I don't think it'll give you much pain."

The pilot wiggled his fingers, twisted his hand.

"Feels fine, Doc," he said. "Thanks. That the worst of the damage?"

"The worst," the other nodded. "You're a tough one all right, captain."

"That's all, Smith," General Horner cut in gruffly. "You can go now. But, remember—don't forget my instructions. I'll have your hide if you ever so much as breathe a word!"

The young medico stiffened and saluted smartly.

"It's not my practice to disobey orders, sir," he said evenly. "You can depend upon me."

"Good!" the senior officer grunted. "Now, run along."

And when the door closed Horner turned to Dusty and fixed him with glaring eyes.

"Well!" he boomed. "You would have to go and do it your own way, wouldn't you?"

Dusty stared at him.

"Eh, sir? I don't understand. Do what my own way?"

"Get yourself killed!" the senior officer snapped.

"Well, thank goodness I didn't succeed," grinned Dusty. "But by the way—you being here, you must know what happened— did the two medicos get down all right? And what about that sergeant pilot who crashed with me? I don't know his name."

Horner snorted.

"Except for a bad case of fright," he said, "Watts and Standish are safe and sound. And Sergeant Collins got off with only a cut on his head. You were the only one killed."

Dusty frowned at him as he detected a strange note in back of the man's words.

"What do you mean, killed, sir?" he blurted out. "I don't follow you at all."

"I mean just what I say, Ayres. You're killed. Here—this was sent out officially over the AP and UP wires over an hour ago."

As he spoke General Horner fished a press dispatch from his tunic pocket, and held it out. Dusty took it, glanced at the typed words, and started violently.

OFFICIAL TO PRESS

Wash. D.C. July 17*** Captain Ayres, Special Emergency Courier, and former flight commander of H.S. Group 7, U.S.A.F., was killed this morning when a plane in which he was a passenger crashed in the Appalachian foothills just west of Nescopeck, Pa. Three other occupants of the plane escaped by parachute, but Captain Ayres went down with the plane and was killed instantly.

The cause of the crash has not been definitely established yet. According to the survivors the craft, which was en route to Washington, where Captain Ayres was to be admitted to the Military hospital for observation as the result of a sudden relapse from previous injuries, was attacked and shot down by enemy aircraft. However this statement is doubted by General Staff as the location of the attack is too far behind the Front. Any enemy planes that might possibly invade that section would have been sighted by scouts. An official investigation is now underway.

The death of Captain Ayres is a serious blow not only to the Air Force but to the country at large, for his record has....

THE DISPATCH continued on for several more paragraphs

about his record. Dusty didn't bother to read them. He simply swore softly and raised questioning eyes to Horner's face.

"What in hell—pardon, sir, but what in hell is the idea of this bunch of tripe? We were attacked! And dammit, Sergeant Collins stuck with the ship! And—"

"Of course it's wrong!" Horner cut in as the words raced off Dusty's lips. "But it's all for a good purpose. Good Lord, didn't you get some kind of an idea at the very beginning? Or did you really think that Watts and Standish found something wrong with you this morning?"

"Then they were a fake?" Dusty gasped. "But what was the idea?"

"The idea," replied General Horner quietly, "was to make it appear, to all those who cared to find out, that you were not fit for active service. In fact, after a couple of days in the hospital it would have been officially announced that you had died.

"But, as usual, fate stuck trouble in your path. And, as usual, you tore headlong into it. Happily enough, though, you saved us time by getting killed two days in advance."

"Just as plain as mud!" Dusty grated, as the other stopped talking. "So may I ask, why my death is so important, just at the moment?"

"You may," smiled Horner. "But I'll not tell you. There is someone else better qualified to explain. Someone else whose death has also been officially announced. Now, just sit still a minute."

With that the Intelligence officer walked out of the room. But before Dusty had time to untangle any of his thoughts, the general reentered. And following close at his heels was a tall, lean-faced man, whom Dusty recognized instantly.

He was Jack Horner, son of the general. Except to a selected few, he was known as Agent 10, star operator of Uncle Sam's Secret Service.

Often had Dusty faced death with Agent 10, far behind the Black Invader lines. And the last time, shortly before the attack on New York, Dusty had seen Agent 10 die—die in his own arms. It had been a bitter moment, and he had pledged revenge to his dead comrade.

But it had been just another one of war's peculiar twists. Death had been cheated, and Agent 10 had lived to escape once again from the Black Invaders.

Now Dusty leaped to his feet, bounded across the room, and gripped the outstretched hand.

"God, but it's good to see you!" he exclaimed. "They told me you had escaped, but—I hardly dared believe them. I—"

He stopped for loss of words. Agent 10 grinned and slapped him on the shoulder.

"Put it down to a miracle and a couple of lucky breaks, kid," he chuckled. "Anyway, I got away, and I'm still kicking. But you, you've been giving me more grey hairs than all the Blacks put together!"

"Me?" echoed Dusty. "Hell, I always come out on top somehow. Built that way, I guess."

"Maybe," grunted the other as his face went deadly serious. "But you came too damn close to being a corpse, in a Springfield gutter this morning, to suit me. And—"

"You heard about that?" Dusty got out incredulously.

"Heard about it?" echoed the other. "I knew it was going to happen—at least something like it. And I tried to get word through to you, but you'd gone to town before—"

"Hey, hey, wait a minute!" Dusty exploded. "Say listen, I've been shot at, and run into, and shot down, and cracked up and God knows what! And it seems that I'm the only one who doesn't know the why or wherefore. Now, for the love of God, let's—"

Agent 10 stopped him with a gesture.

"Keep your shirt on," he said, motioning Dusty to a chair. "That's just what I intend to do right now.

AT LAST General Horner, his son and Dusty all got seated comfortably. Agent 10 leaned toward the Yank eagle.

"Now," he began, "I'll give you the pictures as they came off the reel. To begin with—No, wait a minute. First, I'm going to ask you not to question me as to how I got some of the information. Flying is your secret, and getting information is mine. Right?"

"Right!" nodded Dusty quickly. "Shoot!"

"O.K. There has been offered a reward of half a million dollars, and a high position in the Black command, for your hide—dead or alive! Through certain channels, that we unfortunately tapped too late, the offer of the reward was passed along to the American underworld.

"In short, not only Black agents, but every rat gangster who can pull a gun trigger is after you. After you for the money and all that goes with it. And the reward was offered by none other than our old friend the Black Hawk!"

At that Dusty jerked up straight in his chair.

"The Black Hawk?" he said. "Why you're crazy, fellow. I killed the Hawk over three weeks ago. Shot him down at the New York show. I even landed and saw him die. I—Hell, don't shake your head like that. I tell you he did die!"

"The Black you shot down did die," answered Agent 10 quietly. "But, he was not the real Black Hawk!

"Now wait. Think back, Ayres. Remember the first time you were captured by the Hawk, just before the Duluth show? The time when you and I busted up their hidden static-jamming power plant?"

"I get you!" broke in Dusty breathlessly. "There were five of them—five Black Hawks, and they all looked the same. Sure, that's when I realized why the real Hawk was known as the man with a thousand lives.

"But, there was a slight difference between him and his doubles. He had a tiny V cut in the corner of his right eye. I saw it, and he knew I saw it. That's what made him get tough and start working on me. Gosh, and so—"

"And so you got one of his doubles at the New York attack," finished Agent 10. "I guess you didn't look for the cut, eh?"

Dusty frowned and shook his head.

"No," he grunted. "In the excitement I guess I just took it for granted that he was the real one. Besides, there wasn't much left of his face, anyway, after the crash. I—Say, I wonder if he was the guy that made that crack—and flew that ship?"

Agent 10 leaned forward.

"What do you mean by that?" he demanded.

In a few words Dusty told of the strange message that had come over the radio just before he crashed. Agent 10 and his father exchanged understanding glances.

"Unquestionably!" nodded the younger of the two. "And that is the main reason why we went through this devious method of getting you here—and proclaimed you dead to the rest of the world. As a matter of fact, both things broke about the same time."

"Both things?" echoed Dusty.

"The first was the reward for your hide," replied Agent 10. "As I said, we found out about it too late to nip it in the bud. Through police cooperation we've found the lairs of the under-world's big bugs, in every city in the country. Word has gone out to them that your death by a gangster's bullet or knife will put a rope around all their necks, no matter what member of what gang gets you. It's a special war emergency measure, whereby warning in advance eliminates the necessity of proof of guilt. But, be that as it may, we were afraid that some dog would get you before his leader called him off. And our fears were damn near justified this morning.

"Anyway, to be on the safe side we arranged that fake medical exam. Those two colonels had their instructions, and—"

Agent 10 paused long enough to smile.

"And, I don't think you've made two new friends, Ayres," he continued. "But, the end has been attained, and that's what counts most, now. You are here, and save for a handful of men

56

who can be trusted, you are dead to America—most important, to the Black Invaders."

"BUT WHAT about the other reason?" asked Dusty as the Intelligence man stopped to get his breath. "What's the Hawk and that death ship got to do with it?"

"Plenty!" Horner's son answered in a hard voice. "That crimson plane you saw him flying—is an American plane. And that disintegrating beam is a secret developed by our own Bureau of Scientific War Research!"

"Good God!" gasped Dusty, "then you mean—"

"That the Blacks stole it two days ago, and have been using it against us."

A lump rose in Dusty's throat, and he clenched his fists.

"I should be put against a wall," he grated. "But for me, those last seven ships would still be alive. I knew there was something up, so I thought I'd spring a trap and see what it was all about. Hell, it was a trap all right!"

Agent 10 put a hand on his arm.

"You're wrong, fellow," he said. "You didn't send those lads to their death. Washington H.Q. received your message and relayed it to the Tenth. But that flight was already in the air, doing a practice patrol over that area. Ten couldn't send them any orders because they were not equipped with radio.

"They were all new ships on a test flight, and—well, it was just one of those things. They just happened to be flying in that particular spot.

"The Tenth flight that did answer your relay call was hardly off the ground before they heard your S.O.S. crash signals. So, you see, it wasn't your fault."

"Maybe not," said Dusty grimly. "But it might have been. And I'll square up for those guys just the same. But, about that ship—how in God's name did they steal it?"

"That's a short, but bitter, tale," replied Agent 10. "Because of the deadliness of the thing, and the possibility of injury to those not connected with its development, all of the work was conducted in a secret laboratory near a small town in the mountains of West Virginia. One of our civilian scientists, Professor Shrouder, was in complete charge. He volunteered his services to the Government. In fact, the idea was originally his, so I understand.

"Anyway, he was given four men from the Scientific War Research Bureau, all the funds he required, and told to go to work. All that, mind you, two months before the Blacks declared war on us! A week after war was declared, a couple of aeronautical engineers from the Dayton factories were assigned to him. And just four days ago the first unit was completed. War department tests were to be made the following day. But that night—"

The agent paused and grated a curse.

"I said it was being developed at a secret laboratory," he went on. "But it wasn't a secret. That night Black agents fell upon the place, wiped it out, and stole the plane and its disintegrator beam. When War Department officials arrived the next morning they found only ashes. Those dirty rats had tested the beam to their liking!"

As young Horner stopped talking, a heavy silence settled over the room. It seemed to Dusty that father and son were waiting for him to speak. They both sat frowning at the floor. He was still for a couple of minutes, and then leaned forward.

"And so," he said quietly, "you figure to have a dead man try and get it back, eh?"

Agent 10 shook his head.

"No, Dusty. Two dead men—you and I!"

The pilot grinned at him, put out his hand.

"That's swell," he said. "Let's go—the sooner the quicker!"

AGENT 10 laughed and raised a protesting hand. "It isn't going to be as easy as all that. In fact," his tone grew serious, "I wouldn't lay a nickel on our chances. However, we have one thing in our favor—they won't be expecting us."

"You mean you know where it is?" asked Dusty leaning forward eagerly. "Hell, if you do, why all this chasing around? Let's just barge in and blow it away from them. After what I saw today, I could go for that in a big way."

"And we'd lose the most effective war weapon that we've ever had," spoke up General Horner. "You see, son, only Professor Shrouder knew the secret of the disintegrator beam. Now that sounds funny, but it's true. There is a secret formula that creates the destructive power. Even the Blacks can't find that out, although they have the one unit made.

"However, an associate of Shrouder's, Colgan, worked with him on the early developments, and he believes that with what he knows of Shrouder's early work that he can solve the secret formula if we can only get the thing back. But, as long as the

Blacks have it, we are helpless—and at the mercy of whatever use those devils decide to make of it."

The Intelligence chief paused for breath.

"Of course," he continued after a moment, "destroying it would be tripping up the Blacks. And if we have to, then we will. But, the War Department has given my office the job of getting it back, so that Professor Colgan can carry on from where Shrouder left off."

"In other words," broke in Agent 10. "The Intelligence Department has been put on the spot. In a roundabout way we were responsible for guarding the West Virginia laboratory, yet—mind you, the War Department cautioned us to keep away from the place so as not to excite suspicion. Nevertheless, now that the apparatus is gone, our department gets the blame. See what I mean?"

Dusty understood perfectly. It wasn't the first time that governmental departments had passed the buck to one another. It was just another case of that old army game, which will live as long as there are soldiers and officers.

General Horner was in a tough spot. He had called upon his ace operator, his own son and in turn Agent 10 was calling upon his comrade.

"Yeah, I see what you mean," Dusty said. "And count on me right through. But you didn't answer my other question—do you know where the ship is? Where they keep it, I mean?"

"That's the catch," answered the other grimly. "I do, and I don't. I mean that there is only one place I think they'd keep it, when it's not in the air—at a place near the lower end of Hudson Bay, on the Rupert River. The Devil's factory, we call it."

"The what?" gasped Dusty. "What do you mean? What's the place like?"

"No man has ever found out and lived," came the startling answer. "All we know is rumor. But the place is some kind of a proving ground—like a gun arsenal, radio testing plant, and so forth.

"Anyway, no one, except Blacks of the high command, can get within twenty-five miles of it. We've been banging at it since the very beginning. Nine of our best agents died—died horrible deaths. Four different times, I just barely escaped with my own life.

"But I didn't succeed in breaking through the cordon of steel they've flung around the place. It's guarded on all sides, from the ground and from the air. A fortress, you might call it. Better yet, a fortress of mystery."

Dusty leaned further forward.

"And you mean to tell me that none of our lads have found out anything about it?" he asked. "Hell, that sounds to me like a swell job for bombers."

"And what would they bomb?" replied Agent 10 quietly. "We don't even know what's there. Remember, it's just an area four hundred miles behind their lines. All we know is that no man has found out what's there, and lived. The very fact that it is guarded so closely must mean that it is the place where they develop and perfect their hellish war devices. That's why we call the place the Devil's factory."

"In short, Ayres," broke in General Horner gruffly, as though he felt himself left out of the conversation, "that's the one place they would keep anything as valuable as the disintegrator beam."

Dusty nodded, and switched his gaze back to Agent 10's face.

"And your plan?" he asked.

THE MAN didn't answer for a moment. He sat staring off into space as though searching for an answer. Presently he turned his head and looked Dusty straight in the eye.

"I really haven't any plans, Dusty," he said slowly. "I think the best way to try and get into the place is by air. That's where you come in. And, incidentally, the reason I want you with me—well, you can guess easy enough."

Dusty grinned.

"Sure, and thanks. But, if this place is guarded, why won't they spot us when we slide in for a landing?"

"We're not landing," Agent 10 replied. "It wouldn't be worth the risk. Besides, if we come out of there we'll be coming out in the disintegrator ship—I hope. In other words—"

"We go in by chute, eh?" Dusty finished for him.

"Right," nodded the other. "It's our only chance. It'll be up to you to get us over the place without being seen. And it'll be up to me to lead the way once we're on the ground—knowing their language and customs as I do. But both of us must get the ship—if it's there. How's it strike you?"

"Swell," said Dusty. "Only it sounds to me like a one man job. Why not let me go it alone? If the ship's there, I'll get it.

A KNIFE PROTRUDED FROM HIS NECK.

You haven't entirely recuperated from your last stay in Black territory."

"Forget it!" growled Agent 10. "We're both going, and that's that. Just remember that nine of my friends died trying to crash that place. That gives me a double reason to go."

"O.K., have it your way," Dusty laughed. "But—"

General Horner suddenly gripped his arm. Eyes flashing a silent warning to them both, the Intelligence chief rose from his chair and tiptoed swiftly over to the door. For a second he paused listening attentively. Then with a quick motion he grabbed the knob and whipped open the door. He sprang back with a sharp exclamation.

Unable to see anything because of the chief's huge bulk, Dusty and Agent 10 sprang to their feet and leaped across the room.

The general was staring down at a huddled figure just outside the doorway. It was the young medico who had taped Dusty's wrist. The gleaming handle of an operating knife protruded from the side of his neck, just below the right ear lobe, and the collar of his ward jacket was stained a deep crimson.

For nearly a full minute all three stared down at him, wide-eyed. Then Agent 10 spoke.

"Damn!" he grated. "It didn't work, after all."

Dusty shot him a puzzled glance.

"Meaning what?" he demanded.

Agent 10 didn't answer directly. Instead he shut the door, leaned his back against it and scowled off into space.

"One of them knows!" he said as though talking to himself. "One of them knows that we're both still alive."

"Oh that?" grunted Dusty. "Well, what do we care? That's not going to stop us. Say, by the way, where are we, anyway? What is this hospital?"

"Washington Military," replied Agent 10 absently. "Damn, I would have sworn that no one saw us bring you in from that crash. But someone must have gotten a close enough look to know that you weren't dead—and he killed Smith. Probably when the medico surprised him listening outside the door. Hell, that throws a monkey-wrench in the whole thing!"

MISERY FLOODED the man's face as he spoke. It was also reflected in the face of General Horner. Dusty stared at them both a moment, then touched Agent 10 on the arm.

"I wouldn't say that fellow," he grinned. "After all, our main job is to get to the Devil's factory and recover the crate."

"I know," nodded the other gloomily. "But you see, I had arranged for us to slip out of here tonight, and pick up a plane near the Washington field. But now that that rat, whoever he is, knows we're both alive he'll keep an eye on us. And when we leave he'll send word ahead. Then trust those damn Blacks to figure out what we're up to."

"Well, let's go after him now," said Dusty. "He must be around the building some place."

"We're in the morgue wing," replied Agent 10. "Only young Smith knew that we were here. As far as anybody else in the main hospital is concerned, we're just two stiffs awaiting burial."

To the utter amazement of both father and son, Dusty suddenly laughed out loud.

"Then what the hell!" he chuckled. "That's perfect. Couldn't be better!"

"Good God, what do you mean?" gasped young Horner.

"Just this," said Dusty excitedly. "You once told me that you were an expert at make-up, didn't you? And this is the morgue wing isn't it? Well, you can just fix us both up so we'll look like dead men. And the general, here, can arrange for two coffins to be flown to New York tonight, for burial tomorrow. We'll be in those coffins. Once we're in the plane just leave the rest to me."

"But—" faltered Agent 10.

"Don't you see?" Dusty cut in on him. "It's our one chance to keep playing the dead man idea. The Black who killed Smith will see two coffins going out of here, see us in them, and begin to think he was wrong after all.

"And by the time he's able to check up at the New York end, why should we worry? We'll be way up north tackling the job. It'll be a cinch. Incidentally, we'll hide a chute in each coffin."

Agent 10 gave him a long searching glance. Then slowly his lips curled back in a grin.

"By God, I think you've hit it, Dusty!" Then turning to his father," I agree with Ayres, sir. I can do the make-up job all right. And if you'll get Agents Twelve and Fourteen, they can carry us out. Then we won't have to bother with any of the hospital attendants."

The senior officer frowned, pursed his lips.

"Hum-m-m, it would be just like you two to get away with it," he said. "But, what about the pilot of the plane that'll take you to New York?"

"Get anyone, sir," Dusty replied. "Only be sure he takes his chute along. No—wait a minute. This'll make it even better. Call my unit and order Lieutenant C.B. Brooks to fly down here for the job.

"Curly—that's what we call him—is my best friend in the Unit, and in case the Blacks listen in on your call, it'll make our case stronger than ever. It'll look as though you're letting one of my old gang pay final tribute, and all that sort of thing."

"But this Brooks?" hesitated the general. "Is he—"

"Don't worry, sir," Dusty cut in quickly. "I'd trust Curly Brooks farther than I'd trust myself!"

The Intelligence chief glanced at his watch and nodded—nodded just a trifle reluctantly, Dusty thought.

"Very well," the general grunted. "We'll take a chance. It's now almost six. We'll make the take-off for nine sharp. That'll give us all plenty of time."

He paused, started to say something else, but cut himself off. Then giving them both a long meaning glance, he turned on his heel and strode through the door. As the door closed Agent 10 took Dusty's arm and nodded to another door on the opposite side of the room.

"My stuff's all in there, where I've been hiding out for the last five days," he said. Then with a happy sigh, "But thank God, I'll be leaving soon!"

Dusty chuckled. But it sounded strangely hollow and an

eerie sensation shot through him. A sensation that he did not understand, and merely shrugged off.

But he would have understood that momentary flash of evil premonition had he known of that jet black eye that was watching him through a tiny, hair line crack in the wall, on the opposite side of the room.

CHAPTER 6
COFFIN TRAP

A T EIGHT-THIRTY that night, two poker-faced men in the white uniforms of military hospital attendants carefully carried two coffins out of the morgue and gingerly placed them in an ambulance van. To reach the van they had to pass between a double lane of soldiers and officers drawn up at stiff attention.

Thus was every one permitted a swift glance at the death-chilled figures in the coffins. When they were placed in the van, the lids were laid gently on each. The two attendants closed the rear doors and climbed in front. Then, preceded by a motor-cycle escort with wailing sirens, the ambulance raced across the city toward the military field.

When the field was reached and the doors of the vehicle opened, the attendants took off the coffin lids, and carried each box over to the waiting military transport plane. A tall, helmeted pilot was at the controls up forward, but he did not even turn his head as the dead men were placed in, and the lids resealed.

In the stuffy darkness of the interior of his coffin Dusty relaxed the stiff and aching muscles of his face and grinned happily. It had gone off just as he figured it would.

Anyone who wanted to, had the chance to see them both. And with the perfect make-up job that Agent 10 had done, there couldn't possibly be doubt in any Black agent's mind that two dead officers had passed by.

Yes, it had gone off perfectly. And once the ship got underway a dead man would arise and give good old Curly Brooks, up forward, the start of his life. Then later, when Curly had been pledged to secrecy, he would bail out and two dead men would carry on to the death venture that awaited them far to the north.

Dusty steeled himself and waited for the quivering motion that would tell him that Curly was taking off. But in that dark, self-made prison the seconds dragged by like years. The air grew hotter and hotter, and his back and leg muscles began to ache from their cramped position.

A hundred times he was filled with an almost overwhelming desire to lift up the coffin lid just an inch or so and allow a lungful of fresh air to drift in. But with an effort he curbed the desire. There was no telling who might be looking in the door, or through the cabin window, and with success only minutes away nothing was worth the risk.

Finally, when Dusty's air starved lungs seemed about to burst, the plane trembled violently and to his ringing ears came the faint throb of revving engines. They were taking off.

Realization was almost as good as fresh air. His blood surged

DUSTY WAS HALFWAY OUT OF THE COFFIN WHEN THE PILOT SPUN AROUND.

through his veins, and his nerves tingled with a renewed strength. Then, as he sensed a smooth swaying motion, he chuckled aloud. They were clear of the ground and Curly Brooks was nosing up for altitude. When he leveled off, then would be the time to go into action.

Another eternity dragged by, and finally the motion of the plane told Dusty that they were flying level. Slowly he raised one hand, pressed it against the lid and eased it up enough to get a grip on it. Then working it off to the side, inch by inch, he finally got enough room in which to sit up.

For a moment or so he sat there in the dim light of the cabin interior sucking in lungful after lungful of cool, fresh air.

A slight movement at his side caused him to turn his head. Agent 10 was sliding the lid off his coffin. Reaching over Dusty removed it and grinned at the made-up face of his friend. Then giving him a wink he turned toward the dim outline of the pilot forward.

"Don't get heart failure, Curly!" he called softly. "But, I'm not as dead as I look."

He expected to see his flying pal stiffen violently and whirl around pop-eyed. But instead, the pilot set the robot controls, then reached out and flipped on the cabin lights. Dusty was halfway out of the coffin when the pilot spun around.

A CHOKED exclamation burst from the Yank eagle's throat as he stared at the man. His only resemblance to Curly Brooks was in stature. His face was hard, and sharp featured. And his eyes jet black, gleaming with a cruel light.

Though he was garbed in an Air Force lieutenant's uniform.

Dusty knew instantly that he was not a Yank. And if he needed confirmation, the ugly, snub-nosed automatic gripped in the man's left hand was more than enough.

It was sight of the automatic that made Dusty go rigid. Faintly, he heard Agent 10 groan, but he didn't look at his friend. His eyes were glued on the pilot's face. For about two seconds, they all held the tableau. Then the Black's lips slid back over white, but uneven, teeth and he chuckled softly.

"Rather a surprise for dead men, no?" he hissed at them both. But as Dusty started to move, "Stop—don't move, Captain Ayres. Or you either Agent 10!"

As he spoke the words, "Agent 10," a marked sneer came into his voice, and his finger on the gun trigger tightened. Instinctively, Dusty steeled himself, half expecting to hear the sharp explosion of the gun. But the Black did not fire. Keeping them covered he moved a step or two closer, smirked down at them and absently fingered the vest harness of the chute pack he wore.

"And who in hell are you?" Dusty barked, merely to break the clinging spell of silence.

"Who am I?" the other laughed at him. Then pointing his gun at Agent 10, "You might say that I'm his keeper. He has not once been out of my sight since he was fortunate enough to escape us some three weeks ago. We have not forgotten Agent 10. And my commanders desire to see him again. They desire to, very much!"

As the man paused long enough to indulge in another of his soft, rasping chuckles, Dusty started to speak then shut his lips tight. He bent his head and stared at his hands resting on either side of the coffin, in order to conceal the look he was afraid had leaped into his eyes.

Though he was not sure, he thought that, as the Black talked, he had seen the faint glow of engine exhausts through the window to his right. Unless his eyes had played him tricks another plane was bearing down on them out of night skies.

Who it was he had no way of telling. He could only hope, and in the meantime stall this Black as long as possible.

"… and there are several who desire to meet you again, Captain Ayres. True, the reward will be mine even though I kill you. But, I believe that the reward will be increased if I take you back alive. Do not place your hopes on that, though. One false move and I will kill you both. Kill you as easily as I would a rabbit!"

"Yeah!" Dusty snapped at him. "In the back like you got that medico in the hospital."

The other shrugged.

"It was unfortunate for him that he came upon me when I did not expect him," he answered unemotionally. Then glancing at Agent 10, "Your plan was very stupid, my good friend," he sneered. "Your friends overplayed their part in transporting Captain Ayres from his crash. And once he arrived at your Washington hospital it was easy for me to confirm what my friends had communicated to me—that he was not dead. After that, patience and waiting rewarded me!"

Again Dusty caught the flicker of an exhaust through the

cabin window, and it was all he could do to stop himself from turning his head and looking directly out.

God, if it was only some Yank wondering why a plane was tearing north with all cabin lights on full! If it was, perhaps he might get some kind of a signal through to him—perhaps just an S.O.S. gesture.

As the thought came to him he unconsciously raised his right hand. The Black stiffened instantly and the gun swung dead on Dusty's heart.

"Put your hand down!" he rasped. "Do not forget my words—I will kill you as I would kill a rabbit."

Dusty grinned, but his eyes were agate hard.

"Seeing it's your party," he said, "tell us how the hell you got the job piloting this plane?"

Once again there came the rasping chuckle.

"Did you not suggest in the hospital room, that General Horner order Lieutenant Brooks down here? Well, others took care of the lieutenant—and I reported in his place. A risk, that some one at the Washington field might know the lieutenant—but I was fortunate."

Dusty strained forward, face red with anger under its death-mask make-up.

"By God!" he roared, "if any of you rats harmed Curly Brooks, I'll repay you double, so help me. I'll kill you with my own hands, and love it!"

THE BLACK'S eyes blazed, and he moved as though to slash Dusty across the face with his gun. But he didn't, for at that moment they all saw the silvery shadow that raced in close and went zooming up over them.

With a movement as quick as light, the Black whipped out his free hand and snapped off the cabin dome lights. And in the dim glow of the glimmer lights he held the gun straight in front of him.

"Don't move!" he hissed fiercely. "Don't move, or—I'll kill you both!"

But though Dusty did not move, he barely heard the Black's deadly order. His heart was pounding with trip-hammer intensity, and his brain was filled with dumbfounded amazement. He had had only one glimpse of that silver shadow as it went scudding up. But that one look was all he needed. Beyond all question of doubt, he knew that the strange plane was his own—the Silver Flash III!

The Silver Flash! Who in the name of God was flying his ship? And what were they doing way down here, anyway?

The questions raced through his head unanswered. But though there were no answers, he felt exultant. Some one—some one of the boys was checking up on this plane roaring north with full cabin lights. And he might—He didn't finish the rest of the thought, for just at that instant the radio speaker unit, close by the Black's head, crackled sound—and the voice of Curly Brooks came booming out!

"Hey you, military transport four! Who's the pilot and why are you running with full lights? Check me back at once!"

Dusty inwardly heaved a huge sigh of relief. Curly Brooks

was out there in the Flash, and checking them! He glared at the Black, whose face was twisted with rage.

"Well!" he roared. "What are you going to tell him? Better make it good, because he's the best shot in the army."

The Black didn't answer. Instead he stood rigid waving the gun barrel from one Yank to the other. Dusty heard Agent 10's breath coming in strained gasps but for the first time in hours he, himself, felt perfectly calm and collected.

Sure, the Black might plug them both. But that thought was lost in the relief that Curly Brooks was still alive, and out there circling about them in the night skies. Good old Curly!

And then Brooks' voice came booming through the speaker unit again.

"Military transport four! Land at once! I'll give you one minute to nose down before I open fire. That's relayed orders from G.H.Q., so you'd better land at once."

As the set clicked off the Black hissed something through his clenched teeth, shot one wild glance at the radio set, then fastened murderous eyes on Dusty.

"You will speak to him, Captain Ayres!" he said in a voice that was little more than a whisper. "You will tell him who you are, and that everything is all right. Speak or I'll kill you!"

Dusty snorted aloud, scornfully.

"Kill, is your pet word, isn't it? Well go ahead. Kill me, and my pal out there will get you."

The Black's face almost ceased to be human it became so horribly distorted with rage. The gun bore yawned at Dusty's heart, and the finger curled about the trigger tightened.

"Half a minute to go, transport four!" boomed the radio.

"God, Ayres—the beam ship!"

Dusty just barely heard Agent 10's groaning whisper at his side but realization came like a bomb bursting in his head. God, yes! He had forgotten all about the beam ship! If they died, who would—

"Wait, wait!" he gasped wildly. "Don't shoot—I'll talk to him. I'll do as you say!"

Air whistled out of the Black's lips, and his eyes blazed up in mad triumph. He gestured slightly toward the radio panel with his gun, and moved so that his back was against the side of the cabin. "Then be quick!" he rasped. "And watch your words, my friend. It is never too late to shoot you!"

Dusty didn't even look at him as he legged stiffly out of the coffin, and moved toward the transmitter tube. A wild and desperate thought was taking place in his mind, but he forced a hopeless and forlorn look to his face.

Sliding into the seat, he spun the wave-length dial to the reading of his own ship, the Silver Flash. Brooks had called them on the emergency wave-length, but he did not want what he had to say to go over a general wave-length.

Then, when the red signal light blinked, he put the transmitter tube to his lip.

"This is Dusty calling you, Curly! Snap off your set and beat it. I'm on a special job, and I don't want anyone to know where I am. Counting on you, Curly, to keep mum!"

"My God, you Dusty?" the booming speaker unit cut in on him. "They said that you were killed in a crash. It's on the official bulletin. What the hell's the game? I want to take a hand in it!"

"You got your orders, Curly!" Dusty said in a hard voice. "Snap off your set and clear out. We don't want company this time. Beat it!"

"O.K.!" snarled the radio. "But I think you're all kinds of a bum, Dusty! So help me, I do!"

A moment later the speaker unit clicked off. Dusty groaned loudly, and got slowly to his feet.

"Well, does that suit you?" he mumbled thickly as he slouched forward. "He won't bother us any—"

The rest was lost in lightning-like action. In a flash, the Yank ace straightened up and hurled himself, hands grabbing for the Black's gun. The man cried out and leaped back, jerked his gun clear from Dusty's clawing grasp.

Still moving forward, the Yank crashed into him and slammed him up against the side of the cabin. The Black tried to slap down with the gun, using it as a club. But in that he made his fatal error, for Dusty's hammerhead fist slicing upward struck the fellow's wrist, and the gun went flying out of numbed fingers.

With a pain-maddened bellow, the Black tried to lurch for it, but Dusty's left, already swinging around, crashed into his chest and sent him staggering backward. Almost before the man had started back, Dusty pivoted and went diving across the cabin for the loose gun. Scooping it up, he scrambled over just in time to see the Black hurling his weight against the cabin door.

"Stop, you rat!" he roared.

But mortal fear had keyed the Black into a frenzy, and he flung himself out into the night. Off balance as he was, Dusty nevertheless was able to pump two quick shots through the door, and a wild scream came floating back to him.

Getting slowly to his feet, he rubbed a sore elbow and grinned at Agent 10 who was still sitting pop-eyed in his coffin.

"Come on, dead man!" he said. "Now, we really do go to work!"

CHAPTER 7
MIDNIGHT WINGS

AGENT 10 made no attempt to move. Like a man in a trance, he stared at Dusty. His lips moved but no words came from between them. Then, suddenly, he found his tongue.

"Great guns," he choked. "God, I thought he was going to get you, sure. But that scream—you must have winged him!"

"Don't know," called Dusty as he slid into the seat. "But he's gone, and that's what counts. We'll just have to take a chance on him not getting word ahead."

By now Agent 10 had climbed from his coffin and was dropping into the spare seat beside Dusty. He grabbed the pilot's arm excitedly.

"We'll have to take a chance?" he echoed. "Hell, you don't mean that you're going through with it now?"

Dusty stared at him in amazement.

"Of course we are!" he said. "What's there to stop us? We've got to get that beam ship, haven't we?"

Agent 10 swallowed and nodded.

"Yes, of course," he said. "But good heavens, Dusty, this is no ship to try and crash through with. We wouldn't be able to get enough altitude to get out of their searchlights going over the lines. Besides, our key plan is shot. Didn't you hear that Black? They know we're both alive. Knew it all the time, damn them!"

Dusty grinned and gave him a playful punch in the ribs.

"Hold on," he chided. "It's not as bad as you think it is. Look—see the way the robot's set?"

The agent leaned forward and scowled at the old fashioned solenoid type of plane control. Once set on the intended course, magnetic electric fields, connected by slide solenoid devices to the controls, held the ship on an even keel and automatically counteracted any slight deviation from the course, save when on a vertical plane. At the moment, the fixed compass reading was a few degrees west of magnetic north.

He glanced up questioningly at Dusty.

"It's set for a general northerly course," he grunted, "So what?"

"Simply that our boy friend was planning to fly us right through," Dusty replied. "Fly us right through in a Yank transport! Which means, unless I miss my guess, that the Blacks are expecting this plane to pass over their lines!"

"Perhaps you're right!" exclaimed the Intelligence man. "At least we may be able to get behind their lines without being bothered. Yet dammit, fellow, the idea that they know we are alive gets under my skin. It's obvious that he signaled our plans up north. And when he doesn't show up, well—"

The agent left his sentence unfinished. But Dusty only chuckled more. He had released the robot device, and the thrill of flying was tingling through his hands on the Dep wheel. Added to that was the sense of relief that Curly Brooks was still alive.

"Forget it, kid," he said, turning to Agent 10. "Just think of what's ahead. In the meantime you can be getting those chutes out. And watch your step because I'm going to kill all lights, and fly my own way for awhile."

TWO MINUTES later, though, the darkness into which he had plunged them both was broken by the red signal light on the radio panel winking rapidly. It was on a special wavelength, otherwise the call would have come in over the cabin speaker unit.

He scowled at it a moment, then reached out his hand and slowly turned the wave-length dial knob. And as he reached the halfway recorder, the speaker unit blasted forth with the strangest babbling of sound he had ever heard. The only thing it reminded him of was a barnyard.

He started to turn it off when Agent 10 clamped a hand down on his arm.

"Don't!" the man breathed hoarsely. "That's the radio signal officer at Black G.H.Q. I'd know that rat's voice anywhere."

Dusty almost leaped out of his seat.

"What? Black H.Q. you—"

"Shut up!" hissed the other tightening his grip. "It's in their vocal code. I know a little of it. Maybe I can pick something up!"

The jabber kept up for fully three minutes, and during that time Dusty experienced the tortures of the damned. That Agent

10 was getting some of it, he knew by the way the man's hand trembled, and the sharp intakes of breath. But he dared not ask what it was all about for fear something would be missed. Then finally, the speaker unit clicked off into silence.

"Well, what was it?" demanded Dusty breathlessly. "You understood some of it didn't you?"

Agent 10's fingers were closing on his arm like a vice. He swore softly and shook his arm free.

"Snap out of your trance, kid!" he grated. "What the hell was it all about?"

"Turn back, or go down and land, Ayres!" husked Agent 10.

"Why? What for?"

"They were calling this ship!" was the excited reply. "Calling the Black who should be piloting it. He's to fly at thirty thousand toward some spot I didn't get. They are sending out an escort. Ten pursuits—and the beam ship!"

In spite of himself, Dusty stiffened.

"The beam ship?" he echoed. "You're sure?"

"Positive! It's no use, Ayres. We can't buck that thing. You'd better land while there's still time."

"Sure you didn't hear where we're supposed to meet them?" Dusty countered.

"No. I think they said some place south of the Montreal area. But I could easily be wrong. Their vocal code is extremely difficult unless you're an expert. Our best bet is to land, Ayres."

"And miss this swell chance?" Dusty scoffed, snapping on the dash cowl-light. "Like hell! See that roller map? Well, Montreal area is way the hell and gone northeast of us. All we have to do is veer a bit west, then straight north and smack into this Devil's factory area. We'll miss them by a couple of hundred miles, easy. It's a break we didn't expect. What do you say?"

There was a moment's silence, then Agent 10 nodded.

"All right, you damn fool," he said quietly. "I started out with you, and I'll finish up with you."

"Atta boy!" Dusty crowed. "Now hand me my chute, and climb into yours. No sense in taking chances we don't have to."

ONE HOUR later they were high above Lake Erie and sneaking northward at half throttle like a ghost bird. Far below them was the central theatre of war with its west and east wings stretching to Duluth and the Maine seaboard, respectively. They were too high to see anything clearly, even though the sky was cloudless. But past experience told them both that on the north side of the lake, engine detector units were tuning in on the throbbing beat of their twin power plants, and that soon great pencils of fog and cloud-piercing radium lights would be shooting skyward to "ring" them for the benefit of defending skymen.

The heavy plane was as high as it would go, and for the next half hour it would be nip and tuck as far as success was concerned. But although Dusty knew full well what their chances were, far better than Agent 10, his face was set in grim determination and his hands on the Dep wheel were steady as rocks.

One half hour of blasting hell, and, if luck stayed with them, a chance to crash the unknown after that.

But as the northern reaches of Lake Erie slid past beneath them, not a single beam leaped skyward. Instinctively, Dusty cut one engine to lessen the amount of noise for the ground detectors to pick up.

As for escaping radium cloud-piercing beams, he might just as well have opened up both engines wide, and gained that much more forward speed. There were no streamers of light, and no exhaust flickers from bat patrol planes combing the heavens. It was as though, save for the carpet of dim stars above them, they were absolutely alone in the air.

And that fact sent a tiny chill rippling up and down Dusty's spine. If only one searchlight would leap up their way, he'd feel a lot better. This damn sliding through skies that should, by all rules of warfare, be packed with defense planes, and mobile ground light units, was very sinister.

A thousand times he strained his eyes in all directions, mostly downward, and saw nothing to ease the tension of his position. The Blacks just weren't going to put up a scrap, and that was that.

Then, suddenly, Agent 10 gripped him savagely.

"There—off to the right!" he rasped in a startled voice. "What the devil is it? See there it goes again!"

Leaning toward the right, Dusty narrowed his eyes and peered out into the darkness. At first he saw nothing, and then a yellow light blinked three times rapidly. He could not tell exactly how far away it was, although he judged it to be well over fifty miles.

In a minute it blinked again but this time there were four distinct blinks followed by two long ones. Body rigid he kept his eyes glued on the imaginary spot in the dark heavens. And when there came more blinks at the end of a minute or two he was filled with the eerie conviction that the queer light had drawn considerably closer.

It was still far east of them, and just a shade to the north. But that it was coming closer he was positive, and he unconsciously veered the nose of their own ship in a more northwesterly course.

AGENT 10

Then, as the blinks came for the fourth time, the blood froze in his veins and a startled gasp slid off his lips. There had been just a touch of green in them this time. Just a tiny flicker, but the sight of it sent horror flooding back to him.

"God! I wonder!" he breathed fiercely.

"Wonder what?" came Agent 10's excited question.

Dusty didn't answer. Instead he reached up and snapped on the cabin speaker unit. Then holding his breath, he stared toward the spot where he had seen the blinking light.

Seconds ticked by, more seconds, and finally the light blinked again. Three times it blinked, and with each flash the cabin speaker unit gave forth a short, high-keyed squeak. Had any of them been prolonged, Dusty knew that he would have heard an eerie metallic scream!

"We're in for it now, kid," he said in a steady voice to Agent 10. "Every dime I own bets that that light is coming from the disintegrator beam ship!"

A low whistle was the Intelligence man's only comment. That and a reassuring pressure on Dusty's arm.

"Yeah!" grunted Dusty as though talking to himself. "I think that they've known we were here for some time. That's why they haven't done anything on the ground. Those blinks are to let the other Blacks know that the beam ship is around—just in case they get in the way. And that means—"

"Means what?" Agent 10 asked softly, as Dusty stopped short.

"It means," answered the pilot, "that yours truly has guessed wrong again. In other words, the lad I thought I winged, must have sent word through to his boy friends. And they guessed that we'd take this route north."

"Well, it's been a swell war," grunted Agent 10, as he sat staring at the instrument board.

Dusty shot him a quick side glance and frowned.

"And it's going to be even better!" he got out grimly. "They haven't licked us yet!"

AS HE spoke, Dusty opened up both engines and swung the plane due west. Five minutes later he veered to the north and looked back. When he saw the blinks again his lips went back in a tight smile. The little points of light were southeast of him, and seemed to be no nearer than the last time he'd seen them.

Turning front, he flew a zig-zag course again. Then cutting both throttles, and opening the compensator to kill every trace of exhaust flame, he nosed the ship into a long, gentle glide to the northwest.

Seconds dragged by and his heart pounded against his ribs furiously. Every part of him was concentrated on the game of hide and seek he was playing. Though there was no way of making sure, he was positive that a death trap was being spread about him.

At regular intervals, the speaker unit made little high-keyed squeaks—some long and others short. The more he thought about it, the more he became convinced that the pilot of the beam ship was using the ray's sound as a means of signaling other planes. But, what planes? He had virtually searched every square inch of the heavens, but not one single moving blur had he spotted.

Then, when he had the feeling that he had outwitted his silent pursuers and was gradually drawing away, the blurred carpet of ground beneath him became alive. A great ring of white lights shot straight up past him on all sides.

So suddenly had it sprung into being, that for the moment

he sat frozen to the controls. But as a yammering fire poured down from above, he galvanized into action and belted the controls with every ounce of his strength.

"Grab that floor gun, and hang on!" he bellowed at Agent 10. "Let her rip at anything you see moving. I'm going to try and get clear of this light!"

As he shouted the words, he flung the big craft into a tight power spin, grabbed the wheel with both hands, and jammed his thumbs against the electric trigger trips. Down they went, a hundred metallic streams of death beating against the dural wings of the ship. At the end of three complete spins, he yanked the plane out, and roared toward the western side of the ring of searchlights.

A black shadow tore past in front of him. He kicked rudder and jabbed the trigger trips forward. The twin guns, faired into the center section of the top wing just above his head, chattered savagely, and he had the exultant satisfaction of seeing the black shadow nose up sharply and go cartwheeling off out of sight.

Cursing and shouting aloud he zigzagged this way and that toward the western rim of the light. Though he didn't take time out to turn, he knew by the sound that Agent 10 was fighting off an attack from below.

One half of his brain concentrated on breaking through the ring of light, the other half cursed himself for a blundering fool. He hadn't had a chance from the very beginning. And now that he was caught in the trap, he realized how simple it had all been.

Naturally he hadn't seen any other planes in the sky. They

had stuck high above him, undoubtedly watching him with night glasses. And that signaling from the beam ship had not been to the planes above, but to searchlight units on the ground. While he thought he was easing clear of the beam ship, it had actually been forcing him straight into this damn light trap. And now—

He uttered a savage curse, and wildly flung the plane up on wing to avoid the deadly cross-fire of two Black Darts that had streaked down out of nowhere. As he went rushing into the clear, he suddenly realized that since the searchlights had gone into action he had not heard a single signal from the beam ship.

The thought gave him a clammy feeling, for he knew, at least thought he knew, the reason. With Black planes in the air the pilot of the beam ship would not risk closing in on the Yanks! The deadly ray might strike one of the Darts. And so the great ship was lurking outside the circle of light, ready to make its kill once he broke through.

With a hoarse cry of rage, he hauled the plane around in a wing-quivering turn as the side of the light ring loomed up in front of him. A few more seconds and he would have gone through. But now, his one chance for life lay in remaining within the ring—and battling the fire-spitting Darts that swarmed about him.

Then, as one came thundering in toward him, swerved sharply and blasted a shower of steel into the tail section, the last bit of truth came to him. These twisting, turning devils were not trying to shoot him down. They were endeavoring to cripple his ship so that he would be forced to land. Trying to snip a control cable or two, and hammer the twin engines so that they would conk out cold.

As though Dusty's thought had been spoken aloud, the harsh, rasping voice of the Black Hawk came blasting out of the speaker unit.

"Land, Captain Ayres, and both your lives will be spared! It is impossible for you to escape us. And as it is a matter of honor with me to capture you alive, I offer you your chance. Why continue to be a fool?"

"It's a trick! That damn rat would never take either of us alive. Or if he did, we wouldn't last long. I say, let's go down fighting!"

Agent 10 had left his gun, and was roaring wildly in Dusty's ear. The pilot nodded and thrust him away.

"Of course we're not quitting!" he thundered. "Get back to that gun, quick!"

Snatching up the transmitter tube, he spun the wave-length dial to the emergency reading with the other hand.

"Offer refused!" he yelled. "Come in and try to get us!"

The reply came back to him in a voice that trembled with rage.

"Very well, Captain Ayres. I come to wipe you both out!"

CHAPTER 8
FLOATING CADAVERS

A MINUTE or so after the Hawk had ceased speaking to Dusty the cabin unit gave forth more sound. It was the same, strange babble that the Yank eagle had heard not more than an hour ago. He turned to rap Agent 10 on the shoulder, but the man was already close beside him, eyes glued to the speaker unit and face set grimly.

When the babble stopped short he looked at Dusty.

"He is coming in, son!" he whispered. "He's just ordered all the Darts to quit us and clear out. Hey, what the hell are you doing?"

"Clearing out too!" shouted the pilot, as he flung the plane into a screaming half-roll that made the wings groan aloud. "Never thought that the Blacks would protect me, but they're going to do it this time!"

"Huh?" Agent 10 yelled back, grabbing frantically for support. "What do you mean?"

But Dusty didn't answer. His keen eyes had seen the Darts swinging into a V formation, and he was thundering down straight for the middle of the V. The Blacks didn't realize his crazy action until it was too late.

They tried desperately to spread out and leave him alone in the air. But, for every turn they made, Dusty made two. Speed was in the favor of the Blacks, but Dusty was tops in flying skill. And as they all went plunging through the ring of light the Yank transport was still protected on all sides by a flock of twisting, turning Darts.

The babble that spilled out of the speaker unit shook with rage, and as Dusty plunged through the ring of light he turned in his seat and glanced back. There, a quarter of a mile behind, and considerably above them, was the crimson murder ship streaking down with the fury of a comet. But no yellowish green eye spewed fan-shaped light from the slot in the turret atop the nose. Had it done so, three Black Darts behind Dusty would have become smoking metal.

As that mad-flying Yank raced through the bath of brilliant light and out into the gloom beyond, he hauled back on the Dep wheel with every ounce of his strength, and thumped down on left rudder. For one horrible second the plane refused to respond. Then like a bird shot on the wing it careened up and over.

As the ship plunged downward, Dusty got a flash glance of three black objects racing toward him. For a moment he closed his eyes, waited for those three Darts to slam into him. But when he looked again, he saw them jerk madly off to the side and go whamming past him with bare inches to spare.

A shout of exultation ripped off his lips, and he promptly forgot all about them. So far so good. Now for the final test.

Eyes steady, muscles braced, he straightened out his dive, and pulled the Dep wheel once more into the pit of his stomach. Up came the nose. He caught it half way, leveled off, and as Agent 10 let out a cry of alarm, the transport plunged right back into the ring of light. Head back, Dusty hung grimly to the wheel and riveted his eyes upward, shielding the lower part of them with his free hand.

Two, three seconds whipped by and then the plane rushed into the interior of the circle. At that moment, Dusty gave a shout of triumph. For there, less than five hundred feet above him was the beam ship tearing down in the opposite direction.

It was under side to him, and Dusty knew instantly that its pilot had not seen him double back on his course.

Hands and feet moving the controls, he banked sharply east and slightly downward. As the beam ship tore through the light, he hugged the inside of the ring for fifteen seconds, and then plunged into it for the third time. The instant it engulfed him he cut both throttles, and stuck the nose down in a long, racing glide. Presently, he shot out into the darkness again. Tapping rudder, he veered sharply to the northeast.

TURNING IN the seat, he glanced back. The light circle was breaking up, and each individual beam was beginning to grope about the heavens. One of them actually caught the crimson ship in its glare, but dropped it immediately. But not before Dusty was able to see that the crimson ship was still racing through the skies in the opposite direction from his own plane.

"Worked!" he gasped as he leaned back. "By God it did work after all!"

Hardly had the words left his mouth than the speaker unit babbled forth with Black vocal code signals. Dusty glanced around at Agent 10 just as the man thumped him on the back. Young Horner's face was beaming.

"You fooled them completely," he choked out. "That was the Hawk ordering them to cover the southern side. He thinks you're trying to get back over the lake."

Dusty grinned.

"He would!" he chuckled. "And, I figured he would! Boy,

there is a bit of life in this old crate, after all! O.K., get your breath, kid. It should be clear sailing now."

"Yeah, until we get there!"

Dusty said nothing to that. Now that they had smashed through the last barrier, and the path seemed clear to the mystery area far to the north, a sense of doubt was creeping over him. For, the very thing they were after, the beam ship, was far behind them tearing around through midnight skies.

They were flying away from it—flying north toward a hidden area where both young Horner and his dad believed the Blacks kept their captured ship. But did they keep it there?

Hell, if he only had the Silver Flash under him, he'd take a chance on trailing the Hawk to his lair. But he didn't dare do it with this crate. Luck had been stretched to the limit on the double-back trick. There was no sense in going back and asking for another close call. Yet, hell—He cut off the thought, and put his mental question into words. Agent Ten didn't answer at once. For a minute or two he sat scowling at the instrument board, almost as though he expected to find what he wanted to say printed there. Then finally he spoke, slowly, choosing his words with care.

"My answer is yes, Dusty. And for this reason: I know the Black territory like the palm of my hand. That is, all except this Devil's factory area. I cannot think of a single other place where they would keep the ship. And why? Because I'm pretty sure that area is devoted to experimental laboratories. Naturally they're going to try their damnedest to figure out Professor Shrouder's basic formula for generating the power."

The man paused a moment, before continuing.

"But whether we get that ship or not," came the words with a sudden rush, "if we can tear the veil of mystery from the Devil's factory and get back with what we learn—we'll be accomplishing a great service for our country."

Dusty started to speak, but held his peace as he glanced at the altimeter needle. They were getting too close to the ground for comfort. Bending over, he flipped up the switches, caught the engines and eased the nose up in a gentle climb.

There were still three hundred miles of wild country ahead of them, and he needed every inch of altitude he could get. But, as soon as the ship was climbing smoothly, he turned and fixed his pal with a keen look.

"Never mind the recruiting talk," he said sharply. "Spill it! What's in the back of your head?"

The other glanced at him startled, then slowly grinned.

"No secrets, eh?" he grunted. "O.K. I'll tell you. But remember, it's personal. My best pal in the department—Agent Four—was on the trail of a Black gas secret just after the outbreak of the war. Well, they caught him, and used him as an experiment. They didn't finish him off then and there. The devils sent him back to us to die.

"It was horrible. They'd used a flesh-eating gas, but pumped enough stimulant in him to keep his heart and brain still functioning. Just before he died in my arms, he told me that a Black known as Shan had done it.

"I've been after Shan ever since, and from what little I've

learned, he's up at this Devil's factory. If I find him, he'll never develop another gas, so help me!"

The last words sounded like steel against steel, and Dusty gasped in amazement. Many times had he seen Agent Ten in action, and he thought that he knew all sides of this nerveless man.

But he was seeing a new angle now. Through the man's eyes he could glimpse a seething volcano of almost unbelievable hatred hidden there. Nothing would be able to help this Shan, if Agent Ten did find him!

To break the spell of silent fury that seemed to grip the man, Dusty reached out and slapped his knee.

"O.K., kid!" he said. "Just wanted your views. We're going through for a touchdown, this time!"

WITH THAT, he promptly forgot the Intelligence agent and centered all his concentration on working the plane up through the night skies.

One hour later, the craft was mushing along at thirty eight thousand, its twin engines striving desperately to keep it up in the thin air. And at the end of the next half hour a bit of rapid air-log-distance-less-wind-drift calculation told Dusty that they were a little less than fifty miles southwest of their destination.

Throttling a bit, allowing the ship to sink down, he leaned forward and stared hard at the distant horizon. He could just faintly see the southern end of James Bay. But as he looked to the east, at the point where the Rupert River ribbons off across the rugged wilderness to connect up with Lake Mistassini, he could see nothing but murky darkness.

For a good ten minutes he stared at the surrounding territory. For all he could see he might just as well have been looking down at the frozen wastes of the polar regions. There was not a light anywhere, not even the flicker of a campfire.

Frowning, he turned to Agent Ten, who was also staring down at the place.

"Still think you're right?" Dusty muttered. "Damned if I don't think it would be worth a try at a flare landing. It'll be a hell of a walk back, if we let this crate go."

In the dim light he saw his pal's face go granite. And a moment later he spoke.

"I'm so certain, I'll chance it alone!"

"Like hell you will!" snorted Dusty. "We'll both—!"

He left the sentence hanging in midair as he suddenly saw a shaft of glowing red light belch upward. It was gone almost as soon as it appeared, but the sight of it brushed all doubt from Dusty's brain. Many times had he seen a similar sight when flying over the blast furnaces of Pittsburgh.

Action crystallized in his mind, he promptly cut both switches, and nosed down in a glide. Way back in the Washington Base Hospital, while Agent Ten had made them both up to look like dead men, they had discussed this moment and those to follow.

They had planned to glide in from maximum angle with dead engines. And then, when they were low enough so that the air wouldn't bother them, they were to start up both engines and jump together. In that way they hoped to be drifting down in the darkness, while ground searchlights, or air patrols, went to work on their plane.

In case the plane crashed the resultant fire would destroy it beyond recognition, and any Blacks who found it would believe that its occupants had been wiped out by the flames.

Yeah, that's the way they had planned the thing. And if it went off all right, they would be sitting pretty. But—

Dusty swallowed hard as he experienced a peculiar sensation. Would things go off as they planned? For the second time in as many hours he became obsessed with the feeling that things were too damn quiet below. Though they floated down through inky darkness, he felt that a million cruel eyes were riveted upon them—waiting, waiting for the moment to reach up and snatch them from the sky.

And to top the situation a second or too later something swished by directly underneath him. So close did it come that Dusty actually felt the plane rock in the backwash. Eyes steely, he stared through the cabin window, could have swore he saw a great shadow streaking away from him, and then was not so sure as it seemed to dissolve in the darkness.

For the millionth time the Yank eagle wished he were in the Silver Flash. Then, as the spell passed, he gritted his teeth and savagely held the plane in its downward glide.

Again—quite a while later—another shadow swished by. This time close to the left wing-tips, and through his fingers, Dusty felt the Dep wheel move. Move, just as though some unseen hand had pushed up on the left ailerons. Agent Ten must have felt it too, or seen it perhaps, for he suddenly gripped Dusty's left arm.

NEITHER OF the men spoke a word. There was nothing to say. With their lives resting in the lap of fate, they were sliding down into a mystery area from which only one American had ever returned alive. At such a time no man dares speak his thoughts, for fear that his tongue may betray him. And so those two Yanks sat like statues of stone, aching eyes staring down into the unknown.

Suddenly, for the third time, something brushed passed, but overhead. A split second later the plane jerked crazily in the air, and a loud snapping sound came to them above the whistling of the wings.

Hardly realizing that he was speaking, Dusty gasped.

"We snapped a cable! We've been missing the balloons that hold them up. But now we're down in the cables. Get ready kid—over by the door. I think we're bailing out soon!"

"Ready when you say the word, Dusty," was the steady reply.

Risking disaster, the pilot snapped on the cowl dash lamp for one fleeting second. One look was enough for him to check air distance and the altimeter. Air distance placed them five miles south of the Rupert River, and the altimeter needle told him that they were a little less than seventeen thousand feet up.

Half rising from the seat, he reached out to flip the switches and catch the engine, but his hand froze half way there. At that moment the speaker unit gave forth a terrible scream that was like a death knell in Dusty's ears.

THE DEATH EYE HAD SWUNG DOWN ON THE TRANSPORT

Whirling, he bent toward the window and stared out. He saw nothing, leaned toward the opposite window and choked out a wild cry.

Far off across the heavens a long, fan-shaped beam of yellowish green light was piercing the darkness. It was shining nearly at right angles to the line of their glide. Like an eerie finger, it was sweeping from side to side. Then suddenly, it changed and started swinging up and down vertically.

Fascinated, Dusty watched the phenomenon in the night. Then Agent Ten's hoarse voice snapped him out of his trance.

"The beam ship, Ayres! For God's sake, man, bail out with me!"

Dusty spun around and leaped for the seat.

"No," he roared. "We've got to stick for a moment. We can't go now!"

"Are you mad?" the other thundered back. "He hasn't spotted us yet. Bail out while you have the chance!"

"Don't be a fool!" snapped Dusty as he fumbled with the throttles, and pushed them to wide open positions. "He may catch us by accident, as we go down. I've got to make him go after the plane."

Agent Ten yelled something else but Dusty wasn't listening. Fingers working with lightning-like speed, he lashed the Dep wheel back in a climb position. Then edging out of the seat, he set himself to bolt for the door Agent Ten had already jammed opened, and reached back for the switches. Up he flipped them, and his heart went down into his boots as both engines coughed once and died out.

A quick glance through the cabin window showed the disintegrator beam not more than a mile away, a few thousand feet above them. But it was gradually swinging around in their direction. Like a street sweeper covering every square inch of the pavement with his broom, so was the Hawk sweeping every square inch of the heavens with his death ray.

Jerking his eyes from the terrible sight, Dusty reached to the upper, right-hand corner of the dashboard and swung down the contact handle that hooked in the reserve inertia starter. Then bracing himself he stuck out his left foot and clamped it down on the gear meshing plunger. A wild whirring filled the cabin, and one second later both engines roared into full life.

With a catlike movement Dusty leaped for the door, flung both arms around Agent 10 and let momentum carry them out into crisp, cold air.

"Don't pull yet!" he yelled against the terrific rush of air. "We must drop down a little, first!"

"Right!" came the muffled answer in his ears. "Say when!"

"Pull when I let go of you!" bellowed Dusty.

COUNTING SLOWLY, he stared upward. Far above him he could see the exhausts of the transport cutting red paths through the night. And swinging down on it from the left, was the shimmering beam of light. For a chill moment Dusty thought that its side glow would strike them, but the ray swung far clear and slapped down on the transport.

In the great blaze of light that followed, he saw the transport streaking up in a crazy zoom. About its wings were tangled a mass of thin cable wires, but with both engines wide open the

American craft was ripping through them as though they were merely pieces of string.

Just a flash glance, and then the transport seemed to shrivel up. From the wing-tips inward, and from the tail forward, it grew smaller and smaller in that smoking shaft of yellow-green light. Then, as the terrible ray reached the fuel tanks, what was left of the transport disappeared completely in a great shower of flaming embers which seemed to belch out in all directions and fill the entire heavens.

A second later, the great yellow-green eye winked out and a curtain of inky darkness once more engulfed everything. It was then that Dusty wrenched one hand free and grabbed his rip-cord ring.

"Pull with your free hand!" he yelled. "Hang onto mine with the other. We'll land together."

Agent 10 must have thought of the same thing, for the very instant Dusty pulled his rip-ring, he felt Agent 10 jerk up and away. Desperately, he tried to cling to the hand his grasped. But a strength far greater than his, the strength of Agent 10's chute checking the fall, pulled the hand away, and he went swinging off into space alone.

Two seconds later his own downward plunge ceased as the shroud lines went taut and the vest harness dug into him. Swaying gently from side to side, he flung back his head and stared up into the darkness. He was not sure but he thought he saw the faint whiteness of Agent 10's chute. But with the wind watering his eyes it might have been his own chute that he saw. Cupping his hands to his mouth, he called.

"Ten! O.K.?"

There was no answer. Nothing save the faint snapping of the shroud lines as they twisted his body like a free-swinging plummet. Sucking in his breath, he called again.

"Ten! Are you all right?"

Silence, deep, black and heavy came back to mock him. He tried to tell himself that he had fallen so far free of Agent 10 that the man couldn't hear him. But in his heart he knew that that could not possibly be the case. When his chute opened he couldn't have been more than a hundred feet lower than the other man.

Rubbing the water out of his eyes, he peered again and again up into the canopy of inky darkness—and saw nothing. Something brushed against his opened chute. With a jerk he stopped falling.

Instantly there came a ripping sound, and the next moment he was dropping again, but at twice the speed of his original descent. And he was bearing off to the right, too.

In a flash, he realized that the mushroomed chute folds had fouled on one of the balloon suspended cables, and his weight had ripped it free. At the speed he was falling now his legs would be driven up through his skull when he struck.

His only chance lay in pulling himself up the shroud lines on the split side crimping the folds in—just as a professional jumper slips his chute when he wants to obtain lateral direction.

Reaching up, he curled his fingers about the taut lines, sucked in his breath and pulled himself upward. Hanging by one hand he snapped the other one up and got a new hold. Inch by inch he pulled his dead weight up the lines. To his spinning brain it seemed as though he were falling faster than ever.

The lines cut through the skin of his hands like sharp-edged knives, and his bum wrist felt as though it was going to split in two. His breath whistled shrilly from between his lips, and a conglomeration of spinning balls of colored light danced before his eyes.

But the fighting instinct within him refused to let go. Teeth clenched, he forced himself higher and higher by sheer will power.

And then without warning something smacked up against the bottom of his dangling feet. The shock buckled his knees and he pitched forward on his face.

In the nick of time he released his hands from the shroud lines and flung them out in front of him. It was as though his hands slapped down on a great pin cushion, for a hundred sharp pains shot through his fingers and palms.

And like a battered boxer down for the count of nine, he crouched on his hands and knees, swaying from side to side, mumbling incoherent curses that his stunned brain didn't even know he was saying.

CHAPTER 9
SATAN'S DROME

HOW LONG he remained that way he didn't know. But as reaction set in he slumped down, rolled over on his back and lay there fighting for breath.

It came back little by little and with it a renewed sense of strength. True, he seemed on fire from head to foot, and when he put the palms of his hands together he knew that they were both drenched with blood that oozed from countless jagged cuts and scratches. But one thought was crystal clear in his brain—he was still alive, and still in one piece!

Unsnapping his chute harness, he slipped out of it. He tried to gather in the silken folds, but they seemed to be caught on something in the darkness off to his left. After a couple of attempts he gave it up, and getting slowly to his hands and knees he stared about him.

Black night and silence greeted him. Hopefully he strained his ears for some sound that might tell him where Agent 10 had landed. But as he suddenly thought of his own experience, clammy dread gripped him. Perhaps his pal's chute had also fouled on the cables, and the man had dropped to his doom.

Suppressing a shudder, he started feeling about with his hands. Sharp thorns scratched him, and he had the feeling that he'd dropped into the center of a bramble patch.

The ground upon which he crouched did not feel like ground at all, but more like a bed of sharp stones and bits of glass. As he groped about he suddenly felt what he was sure was a brick. Then he felt another and another, fitted snuggly side by side, and seemingly covered with a layer of broken-up cement.

Moving so as to make as little sound as possible, he wormed his way through the bramble bushes toward the right. Each time he put down a hand or a knee he had to bite his tongue against countless stinging pains. But he kept doggedly onward.

He was sure that Agent 10 could not be very far from him, and he was determined to find the man, even if it took the rest of the night.

Then suddenly, he froze motionless, and strained his ears. His right hand had dislodged a stone, and the stone was falling away from him in the darkness. Tap, tap, tap—each sound a bit fainter than the one before, until it died out altogether.

Cautiously he put out his hand, felt the lip of a crumbled wall, and beyond it—thin air. To see anything was impossible, but as he put his head out through the brambles, he felt an up-draft of air against his face. It was as though he were lying face down on the edge of a cliff.

Wiggling back, he reversed his direction, and a few minutes later he experienced the same thing. A stone fell away from the touch of his hand. But this time there was not the tap—tap—tap sound. There was simply a dull plunk somewhere far below him.

Relaxing, he scowled into the inky darkness and tried to picture his position. But apart from the belief that he was on a bramble bush covered cliff, he could picture nothing.

His wrist-watch said two hours after midnight. Another two and a half hours and it would be dawn. Should he wait for daybreak, or should he try to work his way along this wall-shaped formation of ground?

Rolling over on his back he stared up at the stars, studied them a couple of minutes and guessed that the wall ran in a general east and west direction. Another guess gave him the belief that he was somewhere south of the Rupert River. How far south there was no way of telling. After all that had happened, he might be a good hundred miles south, for all he knew.

But dammit, what had happened to Agent 10?

THE QUESTION burned through his brain. At the very last moment, Fate had knocked their well-laid plans into a cocked hat. Agent 10 was going to take charge once they reached the ground. One of the first jobs was to procure Black Invader uniforms for them both. Another, to stain their faces with stuff he carried in a little make-up pouch cleverly hidden under one armpit. Yeah, and a few other things, too. But now—?

Dusty bunched his fists. For all he knew, Agent 10 might be dead, or perhaps dangling high in the air, with his chute folds snubbed around one of the cables.

If Agent 10 were dead, then it was up to him to carry on alone. But he had to make sure. Yet, in this sea of utter darkness about him, it was a hopeless task to even begin to try and find his friend. At least he'd better wait until dawn when he could see what the hell it was all about.

His mind decided, he settled down as comfortably as his unknown landing place would permit, and started to wait out the remainder of the night. But at the end of a scant two minutes he was mentally forcing his body to remain quiet.

Every part of him quivered with a wild desire to get into action. Any kind of action, just so long as it was action. However, sane judgment made him stay right where he was. He glanced at his wrist-watch every five seconds, and vowed each time that the damn thing had stopped.

Fifteen minutes later he was at the end of his rope. He couldn't stand waiting another minute. He had to do something.

He got to his hands and knees, checked the stars once more, and started crawling through the bramble bushes in an easterly direction. But at the end of perhaps ten or twelve yards, he suddenly stopped short, straightened up and stared up into the heavens to his left.

The faint purr of airplane engines had been caught by his keen ears. And as he waited, the sound grew louder and louder, until it came from directly overhead. Though he stared up until his eyeballs ached, he didn't see a single sign of an exhaust flicker.

That however, did not surprise him. The pilot undoubtedly had his compensator throttle open and was smothering all exhaust flames before the exploded gases met the open air.

But the thing that sent a ripple of excitement tingling through him was the firm belief that the pilot aloft was circling about as though getting bearings before coming in for a landing.

Then suddenly, the engines died out, and there was the faint whisper of gliding wings sliding down through the air. Placing the sound which now came from in back of him, Dusty listened to it coming lower and lower.

A moment later the bushes became silhouetted against a faint yellow glow of light. It seemed that the glow was perhaps half a mile away, and on the far side of a slight rise in the ground.

But Dusty paid little attention to it. His brain automatically figured it as coming from the landing lights of a drome. What interested him more was the moving blur that he could just faintly see sliding down out of the sky.

For several seconds it was just a moving blur, and then as it slid within range of the glow he saw the sleek, crimson wings, the twin propellers, and the queer looking turret mounted atop the fuselage and just back of the nose. The beam ship!

He almost shouted the words aloud. Tense with excitement, he watched the death plane slide down behind a curtain of thin cables, and disappear from sight beyond the rise in the ground.

And then, as he leaped to his feet for a flash glance survey of his own surroundings, the glow of light snapped out, and the blanket of inky darkness engulfed him again. He cursed softly, and called himself a fool for having spent so much time watching the beam ship.

But he hesitated for only a moment. Then he reversed his direction and started crawling westward. The blood pounded against his temples and his hands and knees were raw and pained. But his brain was too occupied with more important things to notice pain.

ONE HOPE of his had come true—he had found the drome of the beam ship. Young Horner and his dad had been right. The Blacks were hiding their deadly prize in the Devil's factory area. And he was in that area. The fear that perhaps he had drifted south of it was unfounded after all. Here he was—maybe right in the very middle of it.

And then, suddenly, as his brain tingled with grim exultation, the ground seemed to fall away from his hands, and he plunged downward into space. Before he was able to realize the danger, instinctive action had made him whip his hands around behind him. Clawing fingers clutched thorny branches, hung on, and checked his fall.

Gritting his teeth against the excruciating pain, he managed to worm backward on his stomach onto solid ground. For several moments he lay there, fighting for breath as great drops of clammy sweat trickled down his brow.

Then slowly, he groped around with his hands, and eventually hooked them over the edge of a stone slab. Inching forward, he reached down and felt nothing but the smooth, perpendicular side of a huge rock. Fumbling about, he found a small stone, and tossed it over. Although he strained his ears, he didn't hear it strike anything.

"Where the hell am I?" he grunted aloud.

The sound of his own voice in the heavy darkness startled him, and he unconsciously wiggled back through the bramble bushes. Cursing his sudden retreat, he checked himself, and lay prone, trying to figure out this new predicament. This did him little good, and brought him even less comfort than had been his before. He was on some kind of a long wall formation that was blocked by a sheer drop to the north, south and west. Perhaps there was a way off the damn thing to the east, behind him. Yet, he was reluctant to turn about and find out. The secret drome with its beam ship was there ahead of him. To the west was where he wanted to go. But, dammit, he—

Perhaps it was just by accident, or perhaps it was that certain thing that science likes to call the sixth sense, but at any rate, he suddenly banished all thought and lay motionless, air clamped in his lungs. Seconds ticked by, rather they dragged by, and then he sensed rather than heard a slight movement to his right. A moment later he heard definite sound, like cloth brushing against cloth—heavy, ribbed cloth. It came from the right, yet to his keyed ears it seemed to come from below his position. And then suddenly it stopped and he heard nothing but the ringing in his ears.

Tingling all over, he inched his body around, and like a mountain panther stalking its prey, he oozed himself over the sharp-stoned ground, and under the thorny brambles, until his groping fingers felt the lip of the wall. Slowly flattening down, he lay as one dead, eyes riveted on the darkness ahead and below.

Perhaps five minutes passed when there came a scratching sound, that to his ears was akin to the roar of a naval gun. A tiny flicker of flame came to life below him and not five feet to his right. But, it was not the flicker of flame that made his heart loop over. It was what that tiny flame brought out in clear relief—the sharp, cruel features of a Black Invader infantryman with a cigarette stuck between his thick lips.

As the man touched the match to it, Dusty could clearly see the rifle slung carelessly over his shoulder, and the ugly, bulb-shaped gas-gun hanging from his belt. And then detail was lost as the Black blew out the match. But the glowing tip of the cigarette remained to mark the spot where he stood.

Here was a bit of luck—here was a perfect chance to get a Black Invader uniform that Agent 10 had insisted they both should have. If only the man would move closer, he'd drop on him, and that would be that. He realized now why the stone he'd dislodged had dropped with a plunk.

In the second allowed, he had seen the partially soggy, moss-covered ground about fifteen feet below him. The place where he now lay must be a wall after all—a wall along the edge of a cliff. He shuddered when he thought of how close he had come to spilling off the side of it.

But he suddenly cut off his silent musings as the glow of the cigarette started to move away from him. Hell, the Black, a guard on patrol obviously, was continuing on his way. Another second or two and a perfect chance would be lost.

Thought and action became one. Picking up a brick over which his fingers were curled, Dusty tossed it straight down in front of him. The sound it made as it hit was like the smack of a cockpit seat cushion against the side of a hangar.

Instantly the glowing cigarette tip stopped moving. Another second and it disappeared. Then there came the soft click of a rifle bolt sliding into place.

HOLDING HIS breath, Dusty slowly braced his legs under him and waited. During the next few seconds it was as though he were in a world of the dead. There wasn't a sound; not even the soft whisper of wind in the bramble bushes.

And then, his straining ears caught the faint scuff-scuff of ribbed clothing rubbing together. It was directly below him. A moment more and he was positive that he could see a blurred hulk crouched motionless. When it suddenly moved, he was sure.

Like a shot his coiled body streaked downward. His out-flung hands smashed into massive shoulders and slid off before he could get a grip. The stillness was blasted by a rasping grunt, as the dark blur jerked violently. And then the weight of his body crashed against it, and air whistled from his lungs.

Fists doubled, he swung blindly as the hulk beneath him crumpled and went sprawling on the ground. Sharp pain shot up his right arm, but his heart leaped with joy as his ringing ears heard a gurgling gasp.

And then the ground seemed to zoom up and pound itself against the base of his skull. His head throbbed and a thousand pin-wheels of colored light zipped around inside. But, subconsciously, he knew that his arms were locked about a struggling figure and he hung on with every bit of his strength.

But he simply closed his eyes, held his breath, and worked his hands upward over coarse cloth. Inch by inch they moved upward, but as a battering ram crushed into the pit of his stomach, and two fingers of steel dug into his eyes, he had to release his grip and jump back.

The moment he let go, a harsh voice, snarled words he did not understand, and before he could brace himself a whirling tornado slammed into him. With a furious effort he jerked to one side, tripped over something—the Black's rifle, his brain flashed—and fell sprawling on his face. But with his surprise advantage lost, he realized instinctively that he was now fighting for his life against an unknown killer of tremendous strength. And so, even as he hit the ground, he rolled quickly to the side and kicked out with both feet. As they smashed into something yielding, his blood danced.

THERE WAS a gurgle to his left. He pivoted and blindly lashed out. Knuckles crunched against bone. Again he smashed, this time with the other hand, and he had the impression that his arm had buried itself in something clear to the elbow. But as he swung again with the other fist, the blurred hulk seemed to clear the ground and fall upon him.

The crushing weight toppled him over flat on his back. Before he struck, steel clamps fastened about his neck. His eyes smarted, and his chest seemed ready to cave in. No matter how he twisted or squirmed, the steel clamps grew tighter and tighter.

His head began to pound and heaven and earth took on the light of day; a light tinged with crimson. He couldn't breath, and his tongue seemed to be forcing the roof of his mouth up back of his eyeballs.

And then, suddenly, the steel clamps fell away from his neck, and the great weight on him went limp. His throat made weird husking sounds as he gulped air into his bursting lungs. Little by little, the crimson glow faded from in front of his eyes and merged into inky darkness.

Then he became conscious of an aching pain in his left arm and right wrist. He tried to move them, but couldn't. They appeared to be locked about the great limp weight that still bore down upon him.

Presently, as his brain cleared, he realized the reason for the strange pain. He had obtained a hammer-lock on the Black, and broken the man's neck. The thought engulfed him, and it was all he could do to push the limp hulk off his chest, and roll out from under it. Presently he pushed himself up on his hands and knees, and began fumbling with the dead man's uniform.

At the moment it was a gruesome task. But finally, not knowing how long it took him, he got the Black's uniform stripped off. And then, after resting a moment, he slipped it on over his own uniform. It was several sizes too big for him, but a perfect fit over his own. That done, he picked up the rifle, but on sudden thought, tossed it aside.

"Too much to lug around," he breathed softly to himself. "My own, and this gas gun will be plenty."

Ten minutes later, he was creeping stealthily across soggy ground, and in the general direction where he had seen the crimson death ship slide down to a landing. The going was painfully slow, and at the end of every ten yards or so he sank down on the ground and strained his ears for the slightest sound ahead. What he might meet between there and the drome he did not know.

All he knew was that somewhere ahead, there in the distance, was a plane that belonged to the U.S.A. On that plane was an instrument of death—an instrument of secret death—that belonged to his country. He had seen it kill; kill his own comrades of the air. It had even tried to kill him. And the man who flew it was his most hated enemy—the Black Hawk. That was more than enough to make him go forward.

Too bad Agent 10 wasn't with him. Too bad his own H.S. Group 7 gang were not with him. But they weren't—that was fact. And there was a job to be done. O.K., he'd do it alone. Do it alone or—

At that instant his crazy, rambling thoughts went flying as a fountain of crimson light belched up into the heavens, perhaps half a mile straight in front of him. Like a giant tongue of flame licking skyward, it flickered for several seconds and then faded out. But the glow it had cast in all directions brought out many things in clear relief to Dusty's straining eyes. He was able to see the double row of low-roofed buildings that ran along the base of a small hill range.

Each was fitted with a tall brick chimney. And it was from one of the chimneys that the belch of flame had come. To the left of the low-roofed buildings, and in the center of a wide valley, he had seen the silhouetted shapes of more buildings. In the seconds allowed, they had appeared to be one story barracks. He instantly guessed them to be living quarters for the Blacks who worked in the chimney-topped buildings.

BUT THE one thing that made his blood dance as he lay hugging the ground, was the memory of what he had seen on the far side of the valley. He had had only time for a glance, but he knew that his eyes had not played him tricks. He had seen the faint outline of the crimson death beam ship, resting with dead props close to a make-shift hangar. And in back of the hangar there was a tiny hut built into the base of a tall radio mast. At least he was headed in the right direction. But he frowned in the darkness as he calculated his chances of reaching that ship. It was beyond the blast furnaces and the barracks; at the far end of the valley and at least a mile and a half away.

To get to it without going straight through the blast-furnaces and barracks, he would have to either skirt the southern side of the hill range, or detour to the north through country.

His watch said exactly four o'clock. Two hours had passed since he had landed on the cliff wall. Another half hour and it would be dawn. Already there was a faint streak of light low down on the eastern horizon.

GENERAL HORNER

One thing was certain. He had to move from his present position. In the momentary glow of the blast-furnace light, he had seen that he was in the middle of a large square of moss and scrub growth-covered ground. In daylight a blind man would be able to see him—and the Black uniform he wore wouldn't help any if others started to get curious. Only a half hour left in which to do something.

Clamping down hard on the tiny tingle of panic that shot through him, he got to his feet and started for an imaginary point to the right of the valley. What he would meet, he didn't know. But, for some reason or other, he felt that it was better than wasting precious time in skirting the southern side of the hill range.

Moving swiftly and silently, he covered a good two hundred yards in the next five minutes. And then, suddenly, as though by magic, a small building loomed up right in front of him. So completely had it been hidden in the darkness that he almost ran into it. As a matter of fact, he actually halted his forward progress by putting his hands against its stone side.

Pausing a second to quell the sudden start it gave him, he then began to inch along to the right. As near as he could tell in the darkness, the building was perhaps twenty feet high. Though he strained his eyes, he could not see either door or window on his side. But as he edged around a corner and worked along another side, his groping fingers touched a barred window. And a moment later, he found himself in front of a small door.

He started to reach out for the knob, when suddenly instinctive alarm shot through him. Were his jumpy nerves playing tricks, or did he actually feel someone close to him? He hadn't heard anything, or seen anything.

Holding his breath, he slowly turned his head and peered into the darkness. Nothing there. He looked the other way, and got the same result. And then, suddenly, a new thought struck him—had he subconsciously sensed the presence of some one on the other side of the door?

Beat it!

The command flashed through his brain. Beat it while he had the chance! How did he know what was on the other side of the door? For one crazy moment he had picked this seemingly deserted building as the place to hold up until dawn. Why, he didn't know. He put it down to a sudden desire to get out of the open. But now, the idea struck him as sheer madness. Hell, he might be walking straight into a trap.

Dropping his outstretched hand, he turned and started to steal away. But he had taken but two steps when something sprang out of the darkness, off to his left, and crashed down upon him.

CHAPTER 10
THE DEVIL'S FACTORY

C AUGHT FLATFOOTED, he didn't even have the chance to swing up a clenched fist before he was felled to the ground by a stunning blow on the side of the neck. Half conscious he flung out both hands and ripped and tore at a squirming weight that was struggling to pin him helpless. And then, out of a fog two half hissed words came to his ears.

"Damn rat—"

Like flood waters bursting over a dam, truth swept through him. With a furious effort, he tore clawing fingers from his neck.

"Ten!" he whispered hoarsely. "For God's sake—stop!"

Instantly the weight on him stiffened, then rolled off as lips sucked in air sharply.

"Good God—you, Ayres?"

Dusty sat up and gulped.

"Yeah!" he got out softly. "Where the hell did you come from?"

A hand found his arm, and pressed hard. Lips whispered words close to his ear.

"Been following you for the last ten minutes. Thought you were a Black. I just got a snap glance at your uniform the last time that blast-furnace shot up flame. Where'd you get it?"

Dusty told him in a couple of short sentences. Then added, "Boy, this helps plenty. Thought you'd gone. I tried to find you, but couldn't. Landed on a cliff wall or something. But, didn't you hear me call?"

"No," came the soft answer. "My chute fouled, too. Hung there for a hell of a while, and then it suddenly let go, and I came down all right. Been prowling around ever since. And then I spotted you, and took you for a Black."

As the joy of meeting his pal again faded away, Dusty leaned close to the blurred figure beside him.

"So what, now?" he breathed tensely. "I spotted where the beam ship is—about a mile up the valley. But, it'll be dawn soon—think we'd better try it?"

There was a moment of silence. Then—

"And what do you think? From what little I've been able to

find out about this place, we're living on borrowed time no matter what we do."

Dusty stiffened at the strained note in the man's voice.

"Meaning what?" he asked. "What have you found out?"

"They know that we're here," was the startling reply. "At least, they know that one of us is here. They found my parachute."

"They?" gasped Dusty as his heart started to do looping tricks. "What do you mean?"

"One of their guard patrols found it," whispered the other hurriedly. "Before I had the chance to hide it, I heard footsteps coming my way. I pulled out fast, then waited. Five of them, and an officer. I saw them in the glow of their flashlights.

"Damned if they didn't stumble over the thing. They scooped it up and went off on the run somewhere. To their H.Q. probably. And, unless I miss my guess, they're going to go over this area with a fine-tooth comb, as soon as it's light enough."

Dusty was too busy with his own thoughts to make any comment at the moment. It seemed as though by some queer trick of fate they no sooner overcame one obstacle than they ran right smack into another and more difficult one. Was it a thousand years ago that they left Washington Base Hospital? Anyway, here they were, virtually within pistol shot of their objective. Yet—perhaps farther away from it than ever.

Dawn was beginning to ooze up. In other fifteen minutes the Blacks would begin to hunt for them. Perhaps the hunt had started already. That they'd find his parachute was a foregone conclusion. And when they did, the Hawk would easily fill in the answers. Dammit, maybe the dirty bum would play safe and fly the beam ship off to some other secret drome.

With that last thought, there came sudden decision for action. He leaned toward Agent 10.

"We'll have to chance reaching that ship," he whispered. "They may get the wind up and fly it away. Got a gun?"

"No," the other replied grimly. "Have you?"

For an answer Dusty shoved the gas-gun in his hands.

"Come on!" he breathed. "Let's go. Stick in back of me and be ready to run for it, if we have to."

THE PRESSURE of Agent 10's fingers on Dusty's arm told him that his pal was ready. Getting slowly to his feet, he started once again in his original direction, toward the right side of the valley. Without bothering to see if Agent 10 stuck to his heels, he went forward at a fast clip, eyes straining through the fading shadows of night.

With each passing second it seemed as though the light doubled in intensity, and that each waving shadow ahead was a Black soldier with his rifle trained on them. But every time it proved to be only a bit of scrub growth swaying gently in a light ground breeze.

Eventually, he saw a small woods to his right. Instinctively, he swerved toward it and increased his pace. The ground was flooded with pale light now, and he could just barely see the blast-furnaces and the barracks, a half mile to the left. And even as he glanced toward them, the still air was shattered by the crack of a rifle, and an invisible messenger of death whined past overhead.

To Dusty, the shot was like the pressing of a hidden key inside of him. In the next second he tossed all caution overboard and broke into a mad dash for the woods. Though he didn't look around, heavy panting told him that Agent 10 was sticking close.

No more shots rang out, and as Dusty plunged into the shadowy shelter of the woods, he breathed the fervent hope that the single shot had been just an accident. And that they had not been sighted. But it was no time to trust in the value of a slim hope, so without checking his speed, he cut sharply to the left and beat a general course up the northern side of the valley.

At the end of a half mile or so, he pulled up short and sank down on one knee. So sudden had his action been that Agent 10 almost fell sprawling over him. In fact, it was Dusty's out-flung arm that saved the man. With a choked gasp, he crouched down.

"What's the idea?" he wheezed. "We'd better keep going. That shot—"

Dusty checked him with a gesture, and pointed ahead.

"Take a look!" he grunted grimly. A dozen yards in front, the woods ended abruptly. And from there on was a smooth strip of ground that led right up to the crimson beam ship resting beside its hangar. On the left were various odd looking buildings. Odd in that they had no windows. Skylights in the slanted roofs served the purpose.

And to the right, and behind the hangar, was the tall radio mast with the queer-shaped building built into its base. And farther back was a long rugged slope of ground covered with heavy undergrowth. A sharp intake of breath caused Dusty to turn and stare at Agent 10. In the dim light the man's face was not pleasant to look upon. His dead-man make-up was smeared all over his face, and tinged with blood that trickled down from a long nasty scratch on his forehead. The American uniform that he still wore was ripped in a dozen different places, and blotched with blood and sticky mud.

In fact, it would take an extra look to make sure that it was an American uniform he wore. But all that, Dusty saw in a glance. What caught and held his attention were Agent 10's eyes. They were like two live coals of fire. As though fanned by the wind, they seemed to actually blaze up and die down with eerie regularity.

Reaching out his hand, Dusty tapped him on the shoulder.

"Snap out of it!" he grunted. "What the hell's the matter with you?"

The Intelligence man didn't even look at him. Simply raised a hand and pointed toward the group of odd-looking buildings off to the left.

"Testing laboratories!" he breathed fiercely. "That's where I'll find that rat, Shan!"

Dusty jabbed him in the ribs.

"Hold it, fellow!" he grated. "One thing at a time—and that beam ship comes first!"

Agent 10 stared at him in a glazed eye sort of way. It was almost as though he hadn't heard. Then slowly he nodded.

"Sorry," he mumbled. "You're right. I forgot for the moment. O.K., you're still leading. Where do we go from here?"

Dusty shrugged, and asked himself the same question. Where the hell could they go from there? On three sides was bare ground, and behind them the woods they'd just come through. It was getting lighter by the second. As a matter of fact, he could see moving figures in the distance. And the beam ship— so near, yet so far. Hell!

THEN, SOMETHING happened that caused him to make up his mind. The door of the small building at the base of the radio mast opened, and the tall, lean figure of the Black Hawk came outside. He paused a few feet beyond the door, lighted a cigarette, and then walked over to the beam ship. Five seconds later, half a dozen mechanics came tumbling out of another building and joined the tall figure.

It was the moment Dusty feared most. The Hawk was making ready to take the beam ship aloft. He grabbed Agent 10's arm and pulled him to his feet.

"Come on!" he grated. "We've got to stop him. Don't know how—but we've got to!"

"Wait, son, wait!" the other hissed back at him. "Look there— to the left!"

Dusty turned and stared in the direction Agent 10 was pointing. Over half a mile away, beyond the testing laboratories, a mass of Black soldiers were slowly spreading out in fan-shaped formation.

One glance and Dusty knew that the search for them was

getting underway. And his heart sank as he saw that they were moving toward the far end of the valley—toward the beam ship.

"See?" came Agent 10's excited whisper. "They've guessed right—guessed that we'll try to get close to the beam ship. Perhaps if we double back we can slip through them, and then wait until they clear out."

Dusty made no reply. He had been thinking the same thought. Like human gates swinging closed, the Black soldiers were slowly boxing in the entire valley and its buildings. Already a detachment was moving toward the woods where they crouched. If they started at once they might slip around the end of the line of searching soldiers and get behind them.

Yet on the other hand, if they hugged the fringe of the woods and moved to the right, with a bit of luck they might be able to dash across a narrow open strip and reach the heavy growth-covered slope behind the radio mast and hangar. In that way they'd at least gain ground. And it would take the Blacks a long time to thoroughly search that slope.

Perhaps it was calm reasoning, or perhaps it was the sight of the Hawk suddenly climbing into the beam ship, that made Dusty make up his mind. Anyway, he shook his head at Agent 10's questioning look, and jerked a thumb to the right.

"We go this way," he said grimly. "If I can only get close enough to plug that rat, it'll be something. We've got to stop him from taking off! We've got to."

The Intelligence man hesitated, frowned, then shrugged resignedly.

"O.K.," he murmured. "Everything's haywire now. One idea's as good as another. Lead on."

KEEPING WELL within the shelter of the trees, Dusty moved rapidly along the edge of the woods toward the right. At that point there was but a sixty yard strip of bare ground between the woods and the shrub-covered slope. He realized that the strip of ground had been cleared as an additional take-off runway for the small field. In fact, it had been so laid out that a ship in the hangar could streak right out on a take-off and its pilot not have to bother about taxiing into the wind.

The very location of the range of hills, and the long slope on the opposite side of the valley, made possible a constant take-off wind from the north. In other words, no matter what the direction of the wind beyond the hill range might be, it was always from the north as far as this small narrow drome in the valley was concerned.

And as Dusty shot quick side glances at it, he noted another reason why the drome had been laid out in a north-south direction. He hadn't sighted them before, but now that dawn was lighting up the earth he could see the maze of cables that stretched high up in the air.

They were spaced about fifty yards apart, anchored to rings embedded in granite blocks, and bowed upward to their mooring balloons aloft. But where the drome was there were none. They stopped abruptly on the west side, and began again on the east side. Thus, the drome formed not only an unobstructed strip between the hills and the long slope, but it was also the base of an air canyon cut through the suspended cables.

Thus a pilot, even at night, had only to hit the area between the hill range and the slope, keep his course due north and he could make a landing without fear of striking the cables.

It was a trick arrangement, but Dusty only gave it a thought. He was mostly concerned with reaching the narrow strip and the wild dash to the slope sixty yards or so beyond. He dared not let himself weigh the chances of getting across without being seen. Perhaps it was because there was nothing to weigh.

In the distance, behind him, he could hear voices calling back and forth to each other—the soldiers of the searching party maintaining contact with their left and right flanks. As he unconsciously quickened his pace, a crazy thought flashed across his brain—he knew now how the fox must feel when the hounds pick up his trail and start baying!

And then, as he reached the narrowest part of the take-off strip, he dashed the crazy thought from his brain and dropped down on all fours. With a grunt, Agent 10 dropped down beside him.

"We'll never make it, Ayres!" whispered the man hoarsely, as he stared out through the shrub branches at the open space. "They're on the far side of the drome now. We'll be in clear view. We won't have a chance. There's still time to double back and slip around to the north of them."

Dusty shook his head doggedly.

"Wouldn't get us a thing," he grunted. "They'd only come back and smoke us out eventually. No sense delaying the risk. Might just as well take it now. Besides—"

The sudden throaty roar of twin airplane engines cut off the rest. Edging forward a bit, he peered around a scrub bush and down the length of the takeoff runway. The twin props of the crimson beam ship were spinning over, and heavy exhaust smoke was spewing backward in the wash.

Flying knowledge told him that the engines would have to be revved up first. By the heavy exhaust smoke, he knew that they were cold, and would require a bit of warming before a take-off. Perhaps five minutes; maybe ten at the most.

Ten minutes in which to reach that plane without being seen!

The ridiculousness of his hopes gave him the sudden desire to laugh out loud. Ten minutes in which to reach that plane? Then what? Just ask the Hawk to step aside and let him take charge? Oh, sure, certainly, the Hawk would be glad to do that little favor for him. The—

He finished the rest with a smothered curse, and turned to Agent 10.

"Sure, I'm nuts, kid," he grunted. "But I'm going to try and reach that ship. Go right through the whole damn lot of them, if I have to. I haven't any plans. Just banking on luck—When we reach the slope—if we do—keep down low and head for the top. That bit of jagged rock up there. See it? Oke. Meet you there in two minutes. An idea just came to me. Maybe we can put one over on these babies, at that. Stop the damn take-off, anyway. Ready?"

Agent 10 started to speak, then closed his lips, and nodded.

"Ready," he grunted a moment later. "You always were crazy, so what the hell!"

Dusty grinned, gave him a playful punch in the ribs, and then wormed out to the very fringe of the woods.

"Here we go!" he called softly. "Zigzag—and run like hell!" AS THE last word slid off his lips, he bent his head down and shot out into the clear. The slope seemed a hundred miles away. Lead weights were tied to his feet, and he wasn't even traveling at a snail's pace. And then as a rifle cracked, his heart seemed to burst inside of him.

The inevitable had come to pass. The searching party had spotted them, and were opening fire. A dozen metallic wasps whined about his ears as he furiously zigzagged this way and that. Twice he stumbled and very nearly fell sprawling on his face, but by a miracle he caught himself in time and kept plunging madly toward the protecting shrub growth on the slope ahead.

Something pecked at the collar of the Black uniform he wore, and little gobs of dust bounced off the ground a bare ten feet in front of him. He thought he heard Agent 10 yell out. But he wasn't sure, and he didn't dare take the time to look back.

All hell was raging about him. The air was filled with the roar of voices and the savage *crack-crack-crack* of rifle fire. He half expected at any second to feel the bite of hot steel ripping into him.

But the hand of the airman's god seemed to be directing those rifle bullets and covering the last ten yards in a wild burst of speed, he flung himself headlong into the scrub growth. The instant he hit ground he was scrambling madly upward.

Branches caught at his clothing and tried to pull him back. But with the fury of an enraged tiger he clawed past them and upward, every second keeping his body low and hidden in the sun-parched growth.

Behind and below him rifles still spat, yet he could not hear any bullets whining overhead. Was Agent 10 still in the open? Were those rats shooting at him? Damn, he was a fool to have let Agent 10 come with him.

It would have been better, perhaps, if they'd split up—if Agent 10 had doubled back so as to keep one of them safe for a little longer. And besides, Agent 10 looked half dead. The man was traveling on nerve alone. He had no damn right to be out of a hospital, anyway.

As a jagged rock loomed up in front of him, Dusty caught short the jangled train of thoughts and stopped dead. Turning around, he slowly stood up and peered through sun-baked branches and leaves down into the valley. The lower end of it was swarming with Black soldiers, all coming forward on the run and firing their rifles blindly in the general direction of the slope.

They were still a good quarter of a mile away, and with a little sob of relief Dusty realized that imagination had played him tricks. At that range nothing short of a lucky bullet could have found Agent 10. In those hellish seconds, he had mentally visualized the soldiers practically stepping on his heels. But, they hadn't been, and Agent 10 must have reached cover.

But, as the seconds dragged by and Agent 10 did not appear, little fingers of dread began to clutch at his heart. The searching party had spread out in line formation and were little more than a hundred yards from the base of the slope. And out of the barracks, across the valley, poured more soldiers, some of them armed with portable machine guns.

A few seconds later, the mighty roar of airplane engines made Dusty jerk his eyes upward. Sweeping up from the south were two squadrons of Black Darts. They, too, had taken up line formation, and their pointed noses were slanted down toward the slope where he stood.

He stifled a groan as memory of Agent 10's words flashed back to him—"No American has ever come back from the Devil's factory alive!" He'd taken it with a grain of salt then, but now he realized how true it must be. By ground and by air, hordes of merciless killers were searching them out. Every element of secrecy was gone now. The Blacks knew that they were there. They had been seen. Hell, living on borrowed time was right!

"God, if he'd only show up!" he groaned aloud. "There's still a chance to fool 'em. Damn, if—"

He stopped short, and choked out a gasp of relief as the shrubs off to his right crackled dryly and Agent 10 plunged close to him. The man was panting hoarsely and fresh blood dripped from the fingers of his left hand. Dusty grabbed him.

"Hit bad?" he asked anxiously.

"Just a nick in the arm," came the tight lipped answer. "I'm O.K. Now what? Stick here and fight it out? Maybe we can last a couple of minutes."

"Stick, hell!" snapped Dusty. "Got matches? Good! Now

listen, you work up the slope, and I'll work down. Set this dried brush afire. The wind will sweep it down toward them. And we'll make a dash for that radio hut down there, under the smoke screen."

And as Agent 10 gulped and started to speak, "Save it, kid. Let's go!"

One minute later the slope was a roaring inferno of flame. A stiff wind whipping up over the crest from the north drove the flames down toward the valley and blanketed out everything in great rollers of heavy smoke.

Above the roar of the flames, Dusty could hear the wild bedlam of shouting below him. And the whine of wings rushing through air told him that the advancing Darts had zoomed up into the clear for fear of running into the cables in the blinding smoke.

His last match used up, he waited a moment in the stifling heat until he saw Agent 10 stumbling down toward him. Then motioning speed with his hand, he turned and started racing down the slope, veering to the right as he went. It was like running through the very pit of hell itself. Countless tongues of flame licked out at him. Soot-filled smoke half blinded his eyes, and the terrific heat seemed to sear his lungs. But shielding his face as best he could, he ran, slipped, stumbled and slid downward.

PRESENTLY, WHEN he was within a dozen yards of where the shrub-covered slope ended and the smooth, level drome began, he jerked to a halt and waited for Agent 10 to catch up with him. Peering ahead, he could just barely see the crimson death ship. It was perhaps fifty yards away. His heart leaped as he saw that its engines had been stopped.

Part of his plan had worked. The Hawk was not going to chance a take-off in the smoke-filled valley. But as his heart leaped with joy, so did it sink with dismay when he saw that a cordon of Black soldiers had been thrown clear around the plane. There were at least twenty of them. Two against twenty—they'd never make it.

Agent 10 must have seen and guessed the same thing, for the man grabbed Dusty's arm and shook his head sadly.

"We might have expected this, Ayres!" he grunted. "They know what we're after!"

Dusty made no reply. In fact, he hardly heard the other speak. His eyes were riveted on the radio shack. A Black soldier was just coming out through the door, and in his hands he clutched a submachine gun.

To that crazy Yank, thought and action became one. He jerked up the automatic he had taken from the Black agent, held it steady for a split second and pulled the trigger. The Black clutching the submachine gun spun around like a top and fell on his face.

The instant the gun had cracked, Dusty grabbed Agent 10 by the arm and started tearing out across the scant twenty yards that separated them from the fallen Black. Oblivious to the hoarse cries that burst from the throats of those about the death ship, he bent over low, scooped up the sub-machine gun on the dead run, pivoted sharply and plunged into the radio hut. A blurred figure spun as he tore inside. He tried to shift the

THE BEAM SHIP WAS POINTED DIRECTLY AT THEM!

submachine gun to his other hand so that he could fire his automatic, but the end caught in the coarse cloth of the Black uniform he wore and made him stumble sidewise.

As he pitched over, he saw the blurred figure raise a snub-nosed gun, and his heart seemed to stop beating. But an instant later there was a sharp hiss close to his right ear, a thin jet of purple smoke streaked passed him and spewed into the face of the blurred figure. He didn't see the man topple over, for at that instant he hit the floor himself.

But up he bounced like a rubber ball, his gun-hand free at last, and his crooked forefinger ready to jerk the trigger. And then, with a grunt, he relaxed and lowered the gun. A Black radio sergeant lay stiff and lifeless on the floor, and Agent 10, the gas-gun still clutched in his right hand, was slamming the door shut. Dusty grinned tightly.

"Thanks, kid. That was close—and how!"

Agent 10 grinned back at him.

"Forget it," he said. "You've done the same for me enough times. Now what?"

Even as the man asked the question, hell-fire broke loose outside and countless rivets smacked against the stone walls of the hut. The glass in the two windows, one on either side of the door, melted into oblivion with tinkling sound, and a burst of hissing wasps zipped through and slapped into the rear wall. Instinctively, both Dusty and Agent 10 threw themselves on the floor, and lay there grinning sheepishly at each other.

Presently, Dusty sat up and glanced at the sub-machine gun he still clutched. There were roughly a hundred shots left in the butt clip. But as he looked about the room he saw a dozen more clips, fully loaded, stacked on a shelf in a corner. He jabbed a thumb toward them and grinned at his pal.

"That'll hold us awhile," he said. "If they try to rush the door, it'll be just too bad."

Agent 10 frowned, and shook his head.

"Hell of a lot of good that'll do us!" he growled. "We can't hold out forever."

"Of course, we can't!" snapped Dusty. "But, you're missing our best trick—our best bet."

"Huh?"

Dusty pointed across the room at the huge radio panel. It was one of the most powerful sets he'd ever seen.

"What do you think that is—a piano? You just keep the door covered, and I'll send out an S.O.S. that'll bring enough bombers up here to blow this damn place off the map. We've done enough for awhile, now we'll let some of the other boys in on the party."

Agent 10 started violently.

"By God!" he gasped. "Never thought of that! I only hope to God they can break through the Black's blockade!"

Dusty snorted, handed the sub-gun to Agent 10 and started to crawl across the floor.

"Wait until you see my gang go to work on them," he said proudly. "They'll take these rats into camp like nothing at all. And we'll—"

He suddenly stopped short, and snapped his lips shut. The firing outside had ceased abruptly, and a booming voice came rolling in to them. It was the voice of the Black Hawk, and sounded as though he were talking through a megaphone.

"Captain Ayres! I advise you both to surrender at once. If you doubt such wisdom, look outside. I pledge my word that you will not be fired upon for the next two minutes!"

For a second, Dusty didn't move. He lay hugging the stone floor and looking at Agent 10. The Intelligence man returned the look with an expression of marked distrust. He even shook his head slightly.

"Don't, Ayres!" he grunted. "He'll plug you, through the window."

Dusty hesitated, clammy beads of sweat forming on his brow. Then with a curse, he got to his feet.

"Got to!" he grated tensely. "I've a hunch what that rat means. And I've got to make sure."

"You damn fool, stay down!" snapped Agent 10.

But Dusty paid no attention to him. Sliding over to the front wall, he edged toward one of the shattered windows. Two inches from it he stopped and braced himself. Behind him Agent 10 was cursing him savagely, but he hardly heard. Two inches more! Dammit, he had to take the chance. He had to get one quick look through the window. He—

"I am waiting, Captain Ayres. I pledge my word not to fire. And I will keep it."

As the booming voice died away to the echo, Dusty sucked in his breath, moved his head forward the last two inches and looked around the corner of the window-jamb. What he saw froze him motionless. If a hundred rifles had opened fire at that moment, he wouldn't have been able to move. His hunch had been right.

There, thirty yards away, was the beam ship. Its tail had been jacked up to flying position. The twin props were slowly ticking over—and the nose of the plane was pointing directly at him!

CHAPTER 11
BLACK ARMADA

THROUGH GLASSY eyes, he stared! A straight into the wide slot in the beam turret atop the fuselage. It was dark inside and he could see nothing. But his spinning brain imagined that he was seeing a smoldering yellow-green eye looking straight back at him.

Absently, he noted that a horde of Black soldiers were grouped together in back of the plane. They were standing in a semi-circle formation that extended back beyond his range of vision on either side. They carried their guns carelessly in their hands, but their bodies were stiff, and every face was turned toward him.

But the one thing he could not tear his eyes from, was the turret slot. To his whirling senses it all seemed like a great red face, and the dark slot was a mouth drawn back in a savage grin. At any moment it would laugh, and horrible death would come spewing out at him.

"Do you understand now, Captain Ayres?"

The booming voice snapped Dusty loose from the paralytic spell that had gripped both mind and body. He jerked back from the window, and turned blazing eyes on Agent 10.

"As I figured!" he said in a voice that seemed to come to his own ears only as an echo. "The beam ship—they've got it trained on us!"

The only change of expression on the other's face was that his eyes seemed to sink back in his head, and the tip of his tongue ran slowly across the width of his bottom lip.

"Guessed it just now, myself," he said slowly. "Well?"

He left the question hanging in thin air. Dusty guessed it and shook his head savagely.

"I'll go to hell before I'll give that rat a break!" he choked out. "Maybe we're done, but by God, I'm going to get word through to the gang. They'll square up for us."

Before Agent 10 could stop him, Dusty darted over to the radio panel, slapped down the power switch and reached for the wave-length dial.

"Thirty seconds left, Captain Ayres! What is your answer?"

"Tell you in thirty seconds!" the Yank roared back defiantly, and spun the dial to the S.O.S. emergency reading.

With the other hand he snatched the transmitter tube from the stiff fingers of the Black crumpled on the floor, and jammed it to his lips.

"All American stations stand by!" he shouted breathlessly. "Emergency! Send bomb and pursuit units to map reading H-27 at once. Prepare to demolish entire area. Strong resistance can be expected. Area must be demolished. Captain Ayres calling! Official S.O.S. orders—send all bomb and pursuit units to map position H-27. Send all bomb and pursuit units to map position H-27! Send all—"

"Ayres!—Ayres!—Ayres! Listen, man—listen—we got a break. We got a break!"

Dusty cut himself off short as Agent 10 pounded him on the back and shouted in his ear. He spun around to shove the man away, then jerked up straight as the thundering clatter of aerial machine-gun fire came blasting down from above. For an instant he gaped stupidly at Agent 10. The Intelligence man was jumping up and down and shouting like a madman.

"Our planes—! Hear them? They've broken through! They're here now, strafing the place. Hear them?"

"Can't be—" bellowed Dusty as he leaped to his feet and raced toward one of the windows. "No one knows where we are—I just sent the message. It can't be—"

He finished the rest in a wild howl of joy as he reached the window. The horde of Black soldiers were scuttling away in all directions, like rats quitting a sinking ship. And slamming down on them, twisting, turning in between the cables, were the boys of High Speed Group Number 7.

In the lead was the bullet-spitting, glistening blur of the Silver Flash III! Tangling with them was a swarm of jet black wings. And with all guns blazing, the air had taken on a great wavy web of criss-crossed tracer streams that blended in with the last wisps of smoke from the dying out brush-fire on the slope.

But as Dusty jerked his eyes down from the glorious sight and looked straight in front of him, a roar of rage burst from his throat. In a flash he spun around, snatched the sub-gun from Agent 10's hands, and went tearing through the door outside.

The instant he hit open air his finger crooked on the trigger and he sent a hail of singing steel zipping after the crimson death ship racing down the runway. But he was too late, and before he could bear down on any vital part, the crimson plane streaked off the ground and went screaming up into the heavens.

An instant later his heart seemed to shrivel up, as he saw the terrible yellow-green beam spew out from the turret slot and start sweeping around toward the 7th gang's ships.

And then, hardly realizing what he was doing, he whirled and raced back inside the radio hut. He crashed into Agent 10, who was gaping at him wide-eyed. Catching himself, he shoved the sub-gun in the man's hands.

"Outside!" he roared. "Get any stray rats on the ground that you can."

And without waiting to see if the man obeyed, he leaped over to the radio panel and spun the wave-length dial to the Group 7 reading.

"Group Seven—Group Seven!" he roared at the top of his lungs. "Keep clear of the crimson plane! Keep clear of that crimson plane. Retreat—retreat! It's fitted with a death beam. Keep clear of it, for God's sake. Stick close to the Darts—it's your only chance. Keep clear of the crimson plane!"

Over and over again he bellowed the warning up into the air to his pals. Above his own voice he could hear the savage clatter of aerial guns. And blending in with it, the rapid bark of high speed antiaircraft guns striving to pick off any isolated

American planes. And then, as a sudden thought crashed through his brain, he reached down and snatched the earphones from the dead Black's head. Before he got them to his own ears he choked out a groan of utter dismay.

IN THE excitement of the moment, he had forgotten all about the possibility of the death beam's screaming sound blotting out his signals to the 7th boys aloft. There in the earphones he could hear its terrible, eerie song now.

Hurling the phones away from him, he leaped up and dashed outside. The sky was gray with archie smoke and tracer streams, but he saw the crimson ship spinning and twisting around to slap its deadly beam down on a Yank plane. Seconds later the crimson ship won and the Yank plane melted apart in thin air and went slithering downward.

A roaring curse of helpless rage blasted out of Dusty's throat, but suddenly changed to a surprised shout as he saw the Silver Flash III come racing down, straight toward the drome upon which he stood. Seconds later it banked sharply away from him, cut around in a dime turn, and slid into a fish-tail landing.

As the wheels braked—sending up little eddies of dust, the glass cowl slid back and Curly Brooks leaped out. His long legs were working like piston rods the instant his feet touched the ground, and before either Dusty or Agent 10 could move, the lanky pilot skidded to a halt in front of them.

"Heard a bit of your voice before the set was blanketed out!" he panted. "Figured you in this hut. Come on—let's get out of—"

He stopped short and glanced at Agent 10 as though suddenly seeing him for the first time.

"Hell, there's not room for three!" he gulped.

"Never mind me!" cut in Agent 10. "You two beat it, while you have the chance."

"Save it!" snapped Dusty, then grabbed Brooks. "No time for questions, Curly!" he rapped out. "Stick with this lad. The rats are too scared to rush you. Most of them have holed up, anyway. See you later."

Curly Brooks stiffened, opened his mouth.

"Hey! What—?"

But Dusty didn't hear the question. He was already racing over to the Silver Flash. Foot barely touching the wing-stub, he vaulted into the cockpit, and rammed the throttle wide open. With his other hand, he shoved the stick forward and kicked rudder hard. Around the plane spun on its right wheel, and then like a shell leaving the bore of a naval gun, it shot forward and streaked up into the air.

The Flash—the Flash under him, at last!

Realization made Dusty's heart leap with joy, and for a moment he forgot about the practically hopeless task that lay before him. But only for a moment did joy rule supreme, for as he jerked his eyes upward he saw the crimson ship tear straight for two American planes. Out shot the terrible yellow-green beam and caught the two Yank planes in its fan-shaped trap. Smoke belched upward, wings melted off and went side-slipping away.

A radial dropped like a stone. A crumpled figure with chute

pack unopened tumbled out of one ship, but the pilot of the other plane did not move from his twisted cockpit. Dusty got a flash-glance of one upraised arm through the greenish black smoke, and then he saw no more as the smoldering fuselage spun earthward like a rocket gone crazy.

The terrible sight seemed to cause something to snap inside his head. A babble of unintelligible words rippled off his lips. He hung the Flash on its prop and spewed hot steel up toward the crimson plane. It was too far above him for any hope of hitting it. But that didn't matter to him now. If he could only attract the attention of its pilot—give the Hawk a chance to see him flying the Silver Flash, then perhaps he could pull the rat away from the rest of the boys.

They had done their job. They had arrived in the nick of time to save him, and Agent 10. Now it was up to him to return the compliment. Undoubtedly, they didn't know what it was all about, and the death ship was melting them out of the air as though they were so many planes made of wax.

"Keep clear, keep clear!" he howled as he saw another 7 plane spin around and charge head on toward the crimson ship.

But even as his wild shout died out to the echo, the deadly beam trapped another helpless victim, and sent it smoking down into all eternity. Banging the throttle and cursing like a madman, Dusty virtually lifted the Flash up closer to the death ship.

His twin Brownings, mounted forward, clattered out jetting streams of flame, and grim joy rippled through him as he sensed that his continuous shower of steel was at last biting through the tail section of the other ship.

147

"Come on—come on, you rat!" he roared aloud. "Try me for a change. Let's see if you can make good this time!"

AS THOUGH at that moment the pilot of the death ship realized that he was being peppered from a blind spot, the crimson plane suddenly slapped up on wing and started to swing down. But Dusty's tensed muscles were waiting for just that moment.

With a lightning-like movement, he slapped the stick forward, then whipped it to the side and jammed on rudder. Down and around under the crimson ship's nose he raced. Then instantly he jerked up his own nose and sprayed the belly of the other ship from props to rudder fin as it thundered past overhead.

"Lousy!" he jeered, as he caught a quick glance of the hawk-faced figure in the cowled-over cockpit working frantically on the controls. "Lousy, you bum. I thought you could fly. Here's some more for you!"

Slapping around, he dived under the tail of the crimson ship, zoomed up and blazed away with both guns at the port engine. That the ship was armored, he had realized the instant his first burst had struck home. He had a savage desire to take a chance and spin over it and down, and blast the glass cowl to splinters and get the man beneath it. But he checked the urge for two very good reasons. As a matter of fact, there were three.

First, because the risk was too great. With the crimson ship under him, there was too much chance of the Hawk nosing up and catching him with the beam. Second, he had seen that there were two men in the ship. The Hawk was aft in the cockpit, but there was a second figure inside the turret. That doubled the risk, because the turret man could operate the beam regardless of how poorly the Hawk handled the plane.

But the third reason for keeping below and out of line of the beam was the most important one of all. That crimson plane was American property. It held one of the greatest secrets of present day warfare.

If the plane were destroyed, then that secret would be lost to America. The death of Professor Shrouder and the others would all be in vain. There would be nothing for Shrouder's former associate to work on—no hope of his carrying on from where Shrouder left off. "Destroy it only as a last resort." Those had been General Horner's orders.

"O.K., general!" grunted Dusty grimly as he stuck right underneath the tail of the other plane. "Just for you, we'll go all the way, or bust a leg doing it."

The Hawk must have sensed Dusty's plan to stick out of range and peck at the engines and tail section, for the plane began to twist and zoom and spin furiously about in the air. But as though he had actually tied the nose of the Flash to the fuselage belly, Dusty hung on steadfastly to his position and pumped burst after burst into the faired-in humps of the twin engines.

"Land, you big tramp, land!" he thundered over and over again. "This time I'm giving you the break!"

But thought of landing must have been the thing farthest from the Hawk's mind, for he continued to hurl his craft about the sky, and all the time the yellow green beam spewed out its fan-shaped ray of death. And when suddenly it clamped down on a lone pursuit plane and melted it into oblivion, Dusty jerked up straight in the seat and yelled in wild excitement. He had got but a flash look at the plane as it went down. But it had been enough to tell him that it was not an H.S. Group 7 ship. It was painted a brilliant orange, and had a large number 5 on the fuselage.

Relaxing for a second, he turned in the seat and stared about him. The sight brought a shout of joy to his lips. There were a dozen Yank squadrons in the air. And low down on the southern horizon, groups of dots were rushing northward.

His S.O.S. call had gone through! The death beam screaming sound had only blanketed out his signals locally. Yank stations had heard them, and now a skyful of eagles were winging their way to battle.

But the joy that was his lasted but a moment. The Blacks had also heard his signals, it seemed. Because from the west and from the east, black wings were racing toward the Devil's factory. And below on the ground, flame guns and archie units were swinging into position to give savage resistance.

And then suddenly, Dusty let out a roar of alarm and flung all his weight forward on the stick. The Flash virtually groaned aloud, and then zipped down like a bullet just as a spear of blistering hell sizzled past above it.

So intent had Dusty been on searching the surrounding sky, that for a moment he had relaxed his vigilance and allowed the crafty Hawk to double back upon him in a lightning maneuver. And only by the very skin of his teeth had he saved himself from being trapped by the death beam.

"You damn fool—you crazy fool!" he howled at himself, and jerked the nose up and cut back in as the Hawk tried frantically to repeat the trick. "Stay awake—where the hell do you think you are?"

The sound of his own blasting voice fired him to a fevered peak, and blotting out everything else from his brain, he tore in and up at the crimson ship. Hammered its tail control-wires section with burst after burst of singing steel. Twice he saw the whole plane tremble violently, and his heart leaped, only to sink down into his boots as the plane slapped around in another wing-screaming effort to get at him.

A thousand other Yank eagles would have been trapped and

destroyed a hundred times over, but each time the deadly beam came within an ace of engulfing him Dusty possessed enough of that natural born airman's skill to skid out of danger, and go zooming up to blast away again at the underneath side of that twisting, whirling crimson blur.

But as he saw his burst of steel rip and tear into the craft, and seemingly do little damage, his hands went clammy on the stick, and hope of complying with General Horner's orders to the letter faded farther and farther away.

Grim fear took its place. Fear that he had over played his hand. And that it was but a matter of time before the Hawk would catch him once and for all. Three times he had actually felt the heat of the beam as it sprayed past him a good fifty yards in the clear. And the memory of it was like a knife twisting in his brain.

What was happening all about him he did not know, nor did he dare risk even a snap glance to see. He kept his eyes riveted to the belly of that ship twisting above him, and simply breathed a fervent prayer that the Yank reinforcements were holding their own with the mighty armada of black wings he had seen streaking toward the area.

And then, suddenly, an unseen hand grabbed at his left wings and jerked back with such a terrific force that he smashed up against the instrument board before he had a chance to fling up a protecting arm. An explosion like that of a gun went off in his head. Balls of light danced before his eyes, and everything became a crazy mixture of spinning blurs.

With effort he forced himself back in the seat, and dashed

a hand across his aching eyes. As sight returned, he stared out at the left wings, and groaned. The Hawk had been playing a game of his own.

Without his realizing it, the rat had forced him down among the cables. At terrific speed he had flown right smack into one of them. In snapping the cable, he had smacked the Flash off balance, and now it was careening crazily down toward more cables.

But even worse than that, the beam ship above was pivoting about, and the sizzling yellow-green ray was swinging down around toward him!

CHAPTER 12
SHAN

THOUGH IT seemed to him a thousand years, Dusty saw and grasped the full significance of the situation in the flicker of an eyelash. The result made his body go cold all over. Yet, at the same time, his brain clicked over at lightning speed. There was one chance. One chance in a million.

Thank God, the wings were not too damaged by contact with the cables. If they could hold out long enough for an outside loop, he could double back under, and perhaps pull the Hawk—

He finished the thought with a mad curse.

"I'll do it, by God!" he thundered. "Damned if I won't!"

Hardly had the first words rushed off his lips than he braced himself with his free hand and jammed the stick all the way up against the instrument board. The Flash quivered from prop to tail, and for one awful moment seemed to buck and refuse to take the controls. Then, like an arrow released from a bow-string, the nose whipped down to the vertical, swept past, and the plane thundered down and up in the bottom half of an inverted loop.

Head thrown back, Dusty caught a glimpse of the crimson plane trying to cut down. Its yellow-green beam sprayed across three cables and they disappeared in mid-air. One, two, three seconds Dusty held the ship steady on the upside of the invert-ed loop. Then he jerked the stick back, jammed on the rudder as best he could and braced himself harder than ever with his free hand.

For a second, nothing happened. The plane kept right on climbing up out of its loop. And the death beam swung closer and closer. Then suddenly Dusty's head snapped back as the Flash corkscrewed in its own length and shot off at a complete right angle to the direction of its loop. Blinded for an instant, he groaned a prayer that he had gauged it right.

Then through a filmy blur he saw a cable sweeping toward him. Kicking over on wing, he skidded around it, dodged to the right of a second cable, and then shot right straight up in a vertical zoom. Seconds later he kicked off the top in a slicing wing-over, cut out into clear air above the small drome and looked back.

What he saw brought a mad shout of triumph to his lips.

"How do you like it, rat?" he bellowed. "A little of your own backwash for you!"

His crazy trick had worked! In a desperate effort to trap his enemy the Hawk had tossed all caution overboard, and had tried to follow through with Dusty's wing-ripping maneuver.

The result was that the Hawk had come down so low that he had trapped himself in the maze of cables. True, the deadly beam spewing out from the turret slot had melted several of the cables. But the wing-spread of the crimson plane was far greater than that of the Silver Flash. Before the Hawk could bank to one side and bring the beam upon it, a lone cable had slapped right smack into the port engine.

In a split second contact had snapped it in two, but the flaying end had wrapped itself about the spinning propeller so tightly that the shaft jammed and the engine died out cold.

With one engine dead, the crimson plane flipped and flopped about in the air like a half-drugged bird. The Hawk, at the controls, tried desperately to hold the nose up, but it was a task too great for a single engine. Little by little the big plane floundered earthward.

"Keep on going down, bum!" Dusty roared.

And as the words raced off his lips, he whipped up in a mad wing-over and went streaking straight down on the top of the crimson plane. Underneath the heavy glass cowl, he could clearly see the Hawk tugging on the stick in a frantic effort to zoom up in a half loop and nail him, but he simply laughed and jabbed the trigger trips. Jetting flame leaped from the muzzles of his guns and sprayed the turtle back of the crimson ship just back of the cowled over pilot's cockpit.

Dusty howled. "Take the break I'm giving you, and land—or it'll be just too bad!"

As though in reply, the crimson ship suddenly banked east and tried to slip through the cable barricade. Once again its deadly beam melted several of them. But again, a lone cable slapped into its wings and threw it over on its side, Sticking close to it, Dusty sent another burst slicing downward, and this time he aimed the burst for a point barely two feet in front of the glass cowl.

"Last call!" he thundered. "The third time you get it, and to hell with the ship!"

AND HE meant what he said, too. Out the corner of his eye he had seen a flight of Darts striving to close in and help their beaten leader. Another minute or so and they would be upon him. Then he would be forced to quit his prize, and save his own neck.

And while doing that, the Hawk would have a perfect chance to limp away on one engine to some point of safety. Last call was right! He could no longer waste time trying to save the death ship. If the Hawk didn't land now, at once, he'd fill his thick skull with made-in-America slugs and let the damn ship crash.

But, perhaps the Hawk did not see the Darts clawing air to his rescue. Or perhaps, Dusty's warning burst brought out the yellow in him. At any rate, however, the death beam suddenly winked out, and the crimson ship went streaking down toward the far end of the runway strip. Right straight for the narrow part that Dusty and Agent 10 had raced across.

Shouting with triumph, Dusty throttled the Flash and slid down after it. It was a tricky job keeping clear of the cables, but to him that part was a cinch after what he'd gone through. Just what his plan would be once the crimson plane touched earth, he did not know.

In a way, it was difficult to plan anything. The Hawk and his partner might stick in the ship, and fight off any effort to capture it. Then again, Dart pilots above might come down and strafe the area so that he himself could not land.

But one thing was certain, anyway. The crimson plane and its deadly beam was all washed up for the present, and it was sliding down to earth. That was plenty for the moment.

Feeding a bit of hop to the twenty-nine hundred horses cowled into the nose of the Silver Flash, Dusty edged in closer, and set himself for a quick fish-tail, windbreak landing, if necessary. With his free hand he pulled the Black agent's gun from the pocket of the coarse cloth uniform he wore and curled his fingers about the butt.

"Half a million dead or alive, eh?" he gritted as he glued narrowed eyes to the crimson plane. "Well, just stick your vulture beak out of that crate, and you'll never make the offer again! Not by a damn sight!"

And then, suddenly, he jerked up straight in the seat and stared down to the left. Like two greyhounds, Agent 10 and Curly Brooks were racing up the side of the drome toward the spot where the crimson plane would touch ground. The Intelligence man was in the lead, and he still clutched the sub-machine gun. Curly Brooks had drawn his service automatic, and he held it pointed straight out in front of him as he ran.

Dusty cursed them both aloud. The darn fools—they couldn't

AGENT 10's GUN FLAMED, THE BIG BLACK CRUMPLED.

possibly reach the ship in time. And even if they did, their very presence would block off any attempt on his part to get the Hawk and his pal from the air, in case they bolted from the ship. He had already shoved his gun back in his pocket, because he had suddenly realized that he wouldn't have time to land and make use of it.

If the Hawk and his pal quit the crimson ship and bolted for the nearby woods, which seemed to be what they were planning to do—he'd have to depend upon his Brownings to cut them down. A slaughter, perhaps, but a couple of dead Black rats, anyway.

The crimson plane was touching ground. Down went the tail, and the craft rolled forward to a jerky stop. A split second later a door on the right side opened and two black uniformed figures leaped out and started racing for the woods. Dusty kicked rudder, swung his plane to the right and stuck the nose down.

"Not a chance, you bums!" he thundered. "Not a—"

He left the rest hanging in mid-air. Rather, he choked it off with a gasp of surprise. To the left, Agent 10 had suddenly cut diagonally across the field, and gained a good fifty yards. In fact, he was so close to the running Blacks that he was practically in line of Dusty's fire, should he jab the trigger trips.

Yet, strangely enough, Agent 10 was not firing his sub-machine gun, though he was within easy range of the two dirt-pounding Blacks. To Dusty, it seemed that Agent 10 was yelling to them to stop.

A moment later he was sure of it, for the smaller of the two

Blacks suddenly halted, spun around and jerked up an automatic. Dusty stiffened.

"Down, 10!" he roared. "Down, and shoot, for God's sake!"

But Agent 10 neither dropped flat, nor pulled the trigger of his gun. Instead, he skidded to an abrupt halt and went through the crazy motions of pointing at his own chest with his free hand.

A SPLIT second later, a flame spat from the automatic in the Black's hand. But, at the same instant, Agent 10 ducked low, and a stream of jetting flame leaped from the muzzle of his submachine gun.

It was as though an unseen fist smashed into the Black's face. His head jerked back, and his body arched. Off balance, he seemed to pivot one full turn on his heels, then over he went on his face and crashed down onto the ground.

As he hit, Dusty snapped out of his trance and kicked rudder savagely. The Hawk had not stopped running, and he was but a few feet from the protecting woods. Cursing, Dusty jabbed the trigger trips and slapped singing steel down at the man. But the god of Hell must have been with the Hawk, because he did not crumple up and pitch forward on his face. In fact, he virtually flew the last few feet and plunged out of sight into the woods.

Jerking his thumbs away from the trigger trips, Dusty whipped the nose of the Flash down, wind-breaking violently and settled to earth a bare twenty feet from the crimson plane. Face twisted with annoyance, he leaped out and ran over to where Agent 10 was toeing over the dead Black.

"You fathead!" he rapped out. "Why did you waste slugs on him? Didn't you know the other rat was the Hawk? I didn't dare fire because you were in line!"

Agent 10 looked up, and his expression was one that made Dusty start involuntarily. A mixture of expressions that included hate, sadness, grim triumph, and a few others.

"He's the one I wanted!" came the surprising words. "And I got him! He died knowing who got him, too, damn his rotten soul. I even gave him first crack—and still got him!"

Dusty grabbed the swaying shoulders and shook hard.

"Hold it, kid!" he barked. "What do you mean?"

Agent 10 pulled himself free and pointed a trembling finger down at the dead Black.

"Shan!" he said, tight-lipped. "I recognized him as he jumped out, and started running."

Dusty swallowed, and nodded slowly.

"Oh, I see," he grunted. Then, "Congratulations."

"Hey, never mind the pink tea! We've got to get out of here fast!"

Dusty turned to stare into Curly Brooks' wide-eyed face. The pilot was pointing excitedly up into the air. He looked up and realized the reason for his pal's excitement. The sky was a solid mass of flashing wings, and most of them were jet black. For every Yank plane that had clawed air north, there were three Black planes to combat it.

American bombers were striving desperately to smack eggs down on the Devil's factory area, but the ground defenses were little short of fountains of flame and bursting steel that spewed up and drove them off. And the few that did break through were being blasted apart by a horde of steel-spitting Black wings.

One look and Dusty snapped into action. He grabbed Curly by the arm.

"Up in the Flash and fly cover over us 'til we get this other crate going!" he barked.

His pal swore.

"You can't, Dusty!" he objected. "It landed with one engine. There's a cable tangled about the prop shaft."

"Can't, hell!" Dusty roared. "Think I'm leaving the thing, now? Get upstairs, pronto, and beat off a strafe if they try it. I'm going to get this thing functioning, if I have to bust a lung to do it!"

Curly started to object some more, but Dusty didn't wait to listen. He simply grabbed Agent 10 and started running over to the crimson ship.

"Move, kid!" he snapped. "Here's what we came up here for!"

Agent 10 had gotten over his spell of triumph and was ready for whatever came next. Without a word of question, he raced shoulder to shoulder with Dusty over to the death plane. But as they reached it and saw the cable coiled about the prop boss and shaft, Dusty's heart sank. It was a job for a couple of mechanics with tools, not one for a couple of men with nothing but their bare hands.

However, grim determination gripped him from head to foot, and he savagely killed all idea of failure at this last moment.

They had suffered too much, and endured too much, to give in now.

"Under the wing!" he snapped at Agent 10. "Hold off any rats that may try to rush us, while I go to work."

WITHOUT WAITING for the other's reply, he dashed around the edge of the wing and in through the fuselage door. It brought him into a short passageway directly between the cockpit and the turret compartment forward. Though speedy action was the one important thing, he could not help but pause and stare at the turret compartment.

It extended like a round cell straight down to the armored floor of the fuselage. Fitted by brackets to the forward wall of the cell was an instrument that looked like a cross between an aerial camera and a gigantic acetylene torch. The camera part was the top—a long telescopic box-shaped snout that extended forward to the edge of the eighteen inch high slot opening.

The acetylene torch part was the bottom—a tall cylinder tank, of some kind of special metal or composition, that extended from the rear end of the telescopic projector down to within a few inches of the floor. About the cylinder were coils of half-inch corrugated pipe, every third coil fitted with what seemed to be a two-way valve. The entire instrument was balanced on the brackets which formed a tripod, and at the top rear of the cylinder were two hand grips.

Thus, the operator could stand up in the cell, grasp hold of the hand grips and swing the beam projector from left to right in the slot. The slot being high up in the turret enabled the beam to clear the spinning blades on either side and the nose of the plane. Dusty noted what looked like rows of mica shields that flanged out from the edges of the slot, and guessed them to be protection against side rays of the beam.

But the thing that held his eye the longest was the control panel, or dashboard, fitted to the bottom right side of the slot. At least he believed it to be the control panel, for he noted that it contained one master switch and a large segmented rheostat unit. After the intricate beam machine, the obvious simplicity of control surprised him.

Up to now one tiny spark of dread had been flickering within him. It had been the fear that even though he captured the ship, he and Agent 10 would be unable to work the death beam. And work it they would have to, if they were to wipe out the Devil's factory. But now—

He cut off the happy thought and ducked back into the pilot's cockpit. A quick movement of his hand to snap off the ignition switch of the port engine, and he was out through the door again, scrambling up on the left wing.

Working forward on the wing-stub, he reached the engine. Its cowling was hot and burned his hands as he crawled over it to the cable snarled about the prop and prop-shaft. But he hardly felt the pain. A terrifically difficult job confronted him, and that was all he thought about.

Sprawling out on his stomach, he tugged at a loose and frayed cable end. About six inches of it came free, but the rest stuck fast. So tight was it wrapped about the prop-shaft, that it seemed to be almost a part of it. And the more he tugged, the tighter it snubbed itself in its own coils.

Sweat poured off his brow and trickled down to smart his eyes. He was dully conscious of the continued roar and clatter of the battle raging in the air above him. And from under the wing came the yammer of Agent 10's sub-machine gun. Even as he heard it, a couple of metallic wasps whined close to him and made sharp popping sounds as they smacked up against the fuselage side to his left.

Instinctively, he flattened himself against the hot engine cowling, but not once did he pause in his frantic effort to unwind the snarled cable and yank it free. Let them shoot, and be damned!

Seconds whipped past and seemingly became an eternity of hellish suspense. His hands were raw and bleeding, and he had tugged only three feet of the cable clear. A shower of bullets sprayed the wing and the ground in front of the plane. Part of his brain was filled with certain belief that the next burst would come slicing down to rip and tear into his back.

He became obsessed with the crazy determination to take the ship into the air with only one engine. The hell with this one! But there was just enough reason left in him to squelch that idea, and make him realize that he wouldn't even be able to get the ship clear. The runway, even with its addition strip, was not long enough for a one-engined take-off.

No, he had to stick and get the prop free, or stay there for the rest of his natural life.

And so with renewed and slightly berserk effort, he tore at the cable and wrenched it this way and that. When one end stuck fast, he wiggled forward and tugged and pulled at the end wrapped about the prop-tips. A dozen times he nearly lost his balance and went pitching headlong over the leading edge of the wing. But each time he caught himself and wiggled back over the cowling.

"Only a couple of bursts left Ayres. And they're coming in bunches, fast!"

Agent 10's shouted warning was like the roar of naval guns in Dusty's head. For an instant he turned and stared across the valley toward the laboratory huts and the barracks beyond. Black troops in prone skirmish position were slowly working their way toward him.

Above, Curly Brooks in the Silver Flash was spewing steel death down upon them. But he wasn't holding them all back. He couldn't, for two Black Darts were forcing him to stop the strafe at intervals and give aerial combat.

And then, as though it were an advance notice of what was to happen in the next few seconds, something tugged at the back of Dusty's tunic and whacked into the armor-plated side of the fuselage. A sense of momentary panic gripped him. With a wild curse he clamped down on his jangling nerves and tore harder than ever at the snarled cable. His fingers were numb with pain and seemed like bleeding stumps attached to his wrists.

Through a clattering fog he heard Agent 10 shout again, but his brain was unable to catch the words. Suddenly, he saw the Intelligence man standing in front of the plane. The man was waving his arms like the blades of a windmill and bellowing at the top of his voice.

"Drop it, Ayres!" he howled. "Drop it! They're going to use their twenty pounders! We'll have to run for it!"

Dusty gulped, snapped his head around and looked across the valley. Agent 10 was right. The Blacks, unable to break through on the ground, were wheeling, a couple of blank-range-fire, twenty pound field pieces up into position. They were less than two hundred yards away.

A second later, smoke puffed out from one of them, and he had the crazy sensation that the ground beneath him had split open, and was swallowing him up.

CHAPTER 13
THE SCREAMING EYE

A THUNDEROUS roar still ringing in his ears, he saw through filmy eyes that the first shell had actually hit about thirty yards off to the left. There was a gaping hole in the ground, and the wing of the plane was covered with a layer of powdered dust.

"Come on, Ayres! Come on you damn fool! The hell with it!"

"Nothing doing!" snarled Dusty, tugging and pulling at the cable. "I'm taking this crate with me!"

His brain tingling with certain expectation that the next shell would blast him out of the war and the world for good, nevertheless he gritted his teeth and stuck to his job. About three quarters of the cable was free, now. Another two minutes and the job would be done.

167

Two minutes! Were there two minutes of life left for him? The question burned across his brain. A roar straight in front of him announced the arrival of a second shell. And the blinding shower of dirt that poured down upon him was definite confirmation. But he didn't even bother to look up, or even duck. One minute to go. Damn his fingers! They were all thumbs.

"Ayres—Ayres! For God's sake, man, we've—"

"Shut up, blast you! Get in the ship! In the turret compartment! We're leaving, pronto!"

As Dusty roared out the order, he called upon every ounce of strength left in him and jerked sidewise and downward on the last coil of the cable. It refused to budge, and then suddenly tore loose as though it were not snubbed at all.

Dusty flung out his hands to save himself, but the momentum of the effort was too great, and he went pitching over the leading edge of the wing and crashed down onto the ground, just as a third shell buried itself in the exact spot where the first shell had landed.

His lungs and eyes clogged with dirt, Dusty scrambled choking and gasping to his feet. Pausing a second to dig knuckles into his eyes and clear his vision, he raced around the wing and virtually threw himself in through the fuselage door. A flash glance as he ducked back to the pilot's cockpit told him that Agent 10 was already in the beam compartment.

"Get it going once we clear!" he roared. "The switch and the rheostat is the—"

"I know, I know!" the other's bellow choked him off. "I've got it figured. Let go, for God's sake!"

By the time Agent 10 had yelled his first two words, Dusty had booted the port engine starter, caught the prop nicely and was taxiing the plane around on one wheel. The instant he straightened out, he rammed both throttles wide open, and prayed.

The prayer was answered. Without so much as missing a single rev the twin engines took all the hop and the plane raced down the narrow strip. Once it swerved crazily as a shell belched up a shower of dirt just off its left wing.

But Dusty's steel grip on the Dep wheel checked it in time. After a couple of dizzy bounces the wheels cleared and the ship nosed skyward. Ducking his head down, Dusty cupped a hand to his mouth.

"Let her go, 10!" he roared. "I'm going to strafe. Watch out for Yank planes!"

For an answer there came a high-keyed whining note to his ears, and the next instant he saw fan-shaped yellow-green light spew out from the turret front. Instantly, he slammed the plane around on wing and shoved the nose down.

The cluster of test laboratories was directly ahead. That is, they were directly ahead for perhaps a split second or two. Swinging the beam from left to right Agent 10 raked the lot, and in a great burst of flame and smoke they melted into oblivion.

Tearing his eyes from the horrible sight, Dusty glanced upward and stiffened in his seat. Racing down toward him was a flight of six Black Darts, their pointed snouts spitting continuous streams of jetting flame. With a lightning-like movement he yanked back on the stick, and pointed the nose up.

"Hey!" came Agent 10's roaring voice.

"Darts!" shouted Dusty kicking rudder. "Get them! Let's see how the rats like it!"

Eyes agate, face grim, he raced the crimson plane straight up into the shower of singing steel tearing down across the sky. And Agent 10 did the rest. Too late the Black pilots realized that their surprise attack had failed. Each tried desperately to wing-over and thunder down into the clear. But Agent 10 caught them square in the beam, and one by one they melted into oblivion.

BY NOW, every Black on the ground knew that the death ship was in the hands of the hated Americans. And as Dusty swung around and down in a wing moaning dive, all hell itself was let loose toward him. It was as though he were diving down into the very vortex of a seething inferno of hell-fire.

The ship rocked and pitched like a rudderless boat in a raging sea. But not once did he pull out. Instead he kept right on thundering down. Up forward, Agent 10 was striving desperately to slap the beam down on archie units and flame throwers, but the crazy motions of the ship were throwing him from one side of the compartment to the other.

"Don't try to swing it!" shouted Dusty, as he saw the beam shoot up and miss the line of blast-furnaces by a good fifty yards. "Just hold her steady, and I'll do the rest!"

Agent 10 must have heard and understood, because instantly the beam stopped moving and spewed out dead ahead. And then Dusty went into action. Using the beam as though it were a mounted machine gun, he maneuvered his plane accordingly. Sawing rudder, he swung the nose from side to side and raked the row of blast-furnaces from one end to the other.

With a roar that made both heaven and earth tremble like wind-whipped leaves, the buildings disappeared in a swirling sea of flame and smoke. Like molten lava from an erupting volcano, the flame mushroomed out over everything within a half mile radius. So great was the explosion, that for a moment the Dep wheel tore itself free from Dusty's grasp, and the plane went skyrocketing heavenward.

"Cut off—cut off!" howled Dusty, as he battled to regain control of the plane. "Yank planes—"

But Agent 10 had also thought of the danger of catching American planes aloft, and before Dusty could finish the warning the beam fused out. Pounding the Dep wheel and rudder pedals, he finally got the ship back on even keel. Instinctively he started to roar into another dive, but checked the maneuver almost instantly.

The work below was finished. There was nothing down there now but an area of raging hell that lapped farther and farther out over the surrounding countryside like blood red waters of a flood tide. Buildings, guns, troops, everything was completely swallowed up in a whirling sea of flaming death.

In spite of himself, Dusty shuddered and tore his eyes away from the horrible sight. The Devil's factory, and its hordes of black uniformed killers were doomed to Satan's charge.

Aloft, however, war still raged furiously and savagely. Every one of the hundreds of Black pilots in the air must have seen and realized that their secret was no more. Yet, rather than discourage them, it seemed to fire their murderers' lust to even greater limits. With reckless, savage abandonment, they hurled themselves down upon their enemies.

Because of the Black's superior numbers American planes began dropping like flies. From horizon to horizon the heavens seemed filled with countless three to one aerial combats—each being three Black killers against a lone, bullet-spitting Yank.

The joyous satisfaction of destroying the Devil's factory area that had been Dusty's, was blotted out by the sight of the aerial slaughter above. And as thought and action became one, he sent the crimson plane zooming up into the raging battle.

"Start up and hold it steady!" he roared at Agent 10. "Don't let it swerve an inch, for God's sake!"

"Steady she stays!" came back the roaring answer.

And as the fan-shaped beam leaped into being again, Dusty hurled himself into the most delicate and dangerous task of his entire career. So great was the chance of wiping out one of his twisting, turning pals of the air, that for a moment he was almost overwhelmed by the urge to slam away and make for the American side of the lines.

Hell yes, wasn't his job done? Hadn't he and Agent 10 recaptured the ship? Dammit, why waste time? Why chance a lucky burst through the glass cowl undoing all that they had accomplished? Sure—

"Like hell you'll pull out!" he roared at himself. "Those lads came to help you. Now, dammit, you help them!"

The shouted words blasting away the urge to retreat, he thumped down on the right rudder pedal and tore straight at three Black planes that were boxing a Group Number 7 plane, and closing in for the kill. Iron grip on the Dep wheel, he edged in and nailed one Black plane. The other two saw what had happened and tried to dive into the clear. A shove on the stick and he caught a second one.

But as he swung toward the third, he groaned in alarm and flung his plane into a screaming dive. The lone H.S. 7th Group plane had slammed down after the retreating Black, and for one hellish instant it seemed as though he couldn't possibly miss flying into the death beam.

As a matter of fact, Dusty closed his eyes so that he would not see one of his own pals die. But as he opened them a second later, a moan of relief gurgled off his lips. By a miracle, he had succeeded in diving the beam away from the battle-crazed 7th buzzard.

CLAMMY WITH sweat, and trembling from the reaction of the hellish moment, he kept the crimson plane in its dive. And then, suddenly, he snorted harshly and thumped his free fist against the side of the cockpit.

"Dummy, dummy!" he grated at himself. "Why the hell don't you use your head?"

Bending over, he cupped his hand to his lips.

"Ten!" he shouted. "Cut it—got a better idea!"

And as soon as the beam winked out he snapped his hand to the radio panel turned on full power volume, and spun the dial knob to the S.O.S. emergency reading. Then he snatched up the transmitter tube.

"All American planes, attention!" he yelled.

And as soon as the red signal light on the dash began to wink rapidly, "All American planes retreat south! This is Ayres in the beam ship. I'll handle them. Get out of my way. Retreat south. All American planes retreat south!"

The red signal light winked rapidly some more, and he knew, or rather guessed, that his pals were trying to contact him for questioning, but he made no move to clamp on the head-phones. He simply repeated his order, and started gaining altitude.

For a few moments he had the impression that his signals had been blotted out, and that the American pilots had not heard. Not one of them broke and started south. As a matter of fact they continued scrapping the overwhelming numbers just as though they planned to stick until they dropped.

Fuming with rage, Dusty cursed them up and down, and repeated his order for the fourth time. But he added a few choice words this time, and with a growl of relief he saw several Yank planes slam into vicious spins and go cutting off toward the south. Presently, the entire Yank armada was clawing air southward. And slamming after them, pointed noses spitting fire, raced the horde of black-winged vultures.

But it was the one maneuver upon which Dusty banked his hope, and with a wild howl he hurled the crimson plane around on wing-tip and whammed right down in among them.

"On, 10!" he thundered. "And hold it steady!"

A high-keyed whine, and the beam spewed outward. Too

late, the nearest Blacks realized that they were trapped. Whether or not they had heard his order to the other American pilots, there was no way of telling. But whether yes or no, the lust to kill had forced them to tear after the retreating Yanks, regardless. And now they were paying for that lust.

Sawing rudder savagely, Dusty swung the nose from left to right and let the death beam do the rest. The result was horrible. Dusty's stomach kicked over the traces, and his mouth went dry as Dart after Dart melted into oblivion. But he did not relent for one single instant.

The memory of the Staff escort and the seven planes of the Tenth Unit was a picture of flame in his brain. And so, cursing and shouting at the top of his voice, he ripped into the skyful of Black wings and sprayed them mercilessly.

Subconsciously, he knew that some of them had skidded into the clear and had circled about and were now flaying his ship from props to tail fin with shower after shower of singing steel. Dully he heard Agent 10 bellowing a warning to him. And through blood-glazed eyes, he saw the engine cowling shake and shiver under the deadly hail of steel.

But in those wild, insane moments he forgot all about his own ship. Let the crackling shower finally break through the armor plating and smash him down. To hell with them. At least the Yank planes were all clear, and now he was paying a debt—a debt to sky pals who had died just as he was making these rats die.

And then suddenly, without any warning, there was a grinding sound up forward, and the death beam flickered out. Instinctively he whipped over in a sizzling half roll and cut downward.

"Ten!" he bellowed. "Don't cut it off, damn—"

"I didn't!" came back the blood chilling answer. "Went off by itself. The tank's empty. Wait a minute! That's right! The discharge gauge is at zero. We're sunk!"

Dusty made no comment. What comment was there to make? The beam power stored in the vertical cylinder had been used up. Obviously the instrument was one that necessitated recharging at stipulated intervals. Why or how, he didn't know. But the fact remained that at the moment of moments the death beam had passed right out of the picture.

And as the truth crashed home to him, he realized for the first time that the ship contained nothing but the death beam unit. There wasn't a single gun in his cockpit or forward in the beam unit compartment. And a swarm of Black killers, who had undoubtedly seen and guessed the truth, were smashing in at him.

Even as he saw them out the corner of his eye, the heavens clattered sound, and a thousand metallic darts smacked into the plane. Jerking his eyes toward the south he stifled a groan. The Yank planes were obeying his bellowed order to the letter, and were clawing away from the area as fast as their thrashing props could take them.

"Hang on, 10!" he roared. "Going to make a run for it—our only chance!"

BEFORE THE last words spilled off his lips, he slammed the Dep wheel over and thumped down with all his weight on the right ruddered pedal. Bullets hammering against its plated sides, the crimson ship seemed to moan aloud as it whipped over, around and down. Head spinning, Dusty clung desperately to the Dep wheel, and counted. At the count of seven, he hauled the Dep wheel back and put on opposite rudder.

For one hellish moment the plane refused to come out of its spin. And then like a shot it went screaming heavenward. Two Black planes directly in its path, darted off to the side as their pilots tried frantically to get clear. But each had forgotten the nearness of the other and with terrific impact their wings tangled and they went skidding off and down.

So sudden and so utterly foolhardy had Dusty's maneuver been, that the swarm of Blacks were caught flat-footed. In fact the very idea of such an unexpected maneuver in that situation was the one thing that saved Dusty's life for the moment.

Like a rocket, he went right straight up through the spinning, whirling fire-spitting mass of Black wings. And the very instant he reached the top of the zoom, he flattened out and slammed the plane into a long, racing dive toward southern skies. But the surprise that had been the Blacks' was but momentary, and like a pack of screaming wolves they went smashing after him. Crouched over the Dep wheel, every muscle in his body tensed to the very limit, Dusty silently cursed the ship onto greater speed.

To his ringing ears came the hellish sound of steel darts biting into the tail section and the turtle back of the fuselage. And the back of his neck crawled with the eerie sensation that already hot steel was smashing through the cowl glass and digging into him. But he made no move to pull his crazy maneuver again. Luck had been with him once. He'd be a fool to chance it a second time.

Speed was his only hope now. Nothing else but speed. And if that failed, well—"Don't think about it, you fool!" he snarled at himself. "Don't think of it!" But his words were only a waste of breath. The thought stuck in his brain. As he sensed, rather than heard, the deadly hail of steel move up the turtle back of the fuselage, dread began to curl about his heart and squeeze tighter and tighter. Any minute, now!—any minute now, and he would hear the tinkle of the glass cowl as the hand of death smashed through to touch him.

But, it was not the tinkle of broken glass that he heard a moment later. Instead it was the roaring voice of Agent 10. "Another break for us, Ayres! Another break. Your gang has come back! By God, we'll make it yet!"

The shouted words made Dusty jerk up his head. Through filmed eyes he saw fifteen planes of the Seventh Group go slamming down into the swarm of air-clawing Darts. And in the lead was Curly Brooks in the Silver Flash III.

Good old Number Seven! The gang had obeyed his order, but they had also kept an eye on him. And now that he was in trouble, racing with death itself, they had returned to make damn sure that their ace of aces won that race.

Like men gone completely mad, the Number Seven gang piled into the Blacks with a savageness that brought a gasp from Dusty's lips. But it must have brought more than just a gasp from the lips of the Black pilots who got in their line of fire. Like the shutting off of a water faucet the hail of steel stopped beating against Dusty's plane. It was turned, instead, on the zooming, spinning and rolling ships of the Seventh gang.

But, as far as those crazy eagles were concerned, the hail of steel was just so many powder puffs to them. Outnumbered though they were, they ripped and tore in like fifteen metallic demons, and in the matter of less than a minute the Blacks began to give air.

That only served to increase the intensity of the American attack. Into that swarm of black wings they tore harder and more furiously than ever. Presently, Black morale broke entirely, and like frightened sparrows they busted apart and went racing away toward the east. Number Seven followed them for a few miles, smacked a couple for good measure, and then swung back and took up escort position around Dusty's plane.

Across the air space he saw the grinning face of Curly Brooks and the rest of the boys. And in that moment his heart seemed ready to explode with pride. Good old Seven—the best damn brood of scrapping, north, east, south and west of anywhere.

THE REST of the flight south was a sort of crazy dream chocked full of conflicting emotions. He cursed some, laughed some, and babbled to himself in between times.

With hands steady on the controls, he sticked the crimson plane down to a gentle landing, less than a dozen yards from the hangar line.

Half falling out of the seat, he stumbled forward and climbed out the fuselage door. His first impression was that everyone in the world was crowding about the ship. Hands grabbed him, and voices shouted in his ears.

But he ignored them all, shouldered through the shouting mob and ran over to where the Silver Flash was braking to an easy stop. And as Curly legged out and grinned Dusty grabbed him by the shoulders.

"Thanks, kid, thanks!" he choked out. "But tell me—now I've got time to ask you—how the hell did you know I was up there?"

Curly Brooks' grin widened.

"Simple," he said. "Remember when you ordered me to beat it, last night? Well, I didn't. I knew something was wrong. You see I'd received word that I was to fly a couple of dead men to New York. But before I got started somebody socked me and I passed out.

"When I came to, I took your ship. At Washington, Horner damn near fainted. Said something about a spy must be at the controls. So I went looking for you, and found you in a crate with all lights on."

"Oh, then Horner told you where we were headed?" grunted Dusty as the other stopped.

"Nope," said Curly shaking his head. "He simply said that you and Agent 10 were dead, and that an unknown pilot, a spy probably, was flying you to New York. I didn't get half what he said, he was so excited and jabbering so fast. Nope, he didn't tell me where you were headed. This did!"

Brooks held up his doubled fist. Dusty frowned, shot a questioning glance.

"Huh? What do you mean?"

180

"Said I stuck around, didn't I?" Curly answered. "Well, I saw that guy jump, followed him down, and caught him. And then—well, guess I got kinda rough, but he told me enough before I eased up. Just a bum who couldn't take it, if you know what I mean."

Dusty nodded and grinned at Agent 10 who had joined them.

"Do we buy him a drink, kid, or do we buy him a drink?"

"Just give me time to see that the ship is turned over to the department," the Intelligence man chuckled, "and we'll split a case among us!"

POPULAR PUBLICATIONS
HERO PULPS

LOOK FOR MORE SOON!

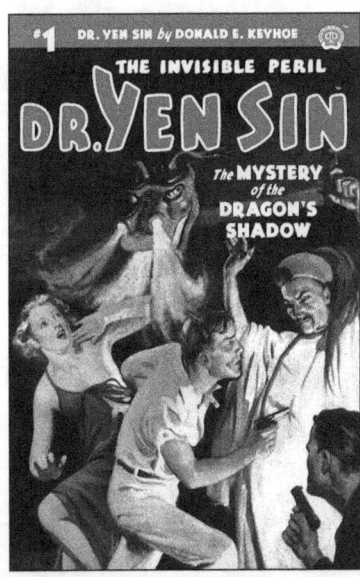

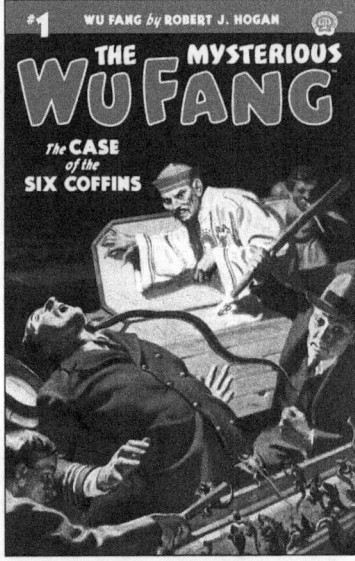